Dickens Advent Reader

Special 24-Day Advent Reader

Dickens Advent Reader

Special 24-Day Advent Reader

Charles Dickens

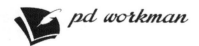

Copyright © 2015

All rights reserved. The study tools in this book are copyrighted and may not be reproduced, stored in retrieval system, copied in any form or by any means, electronic, mechanical, photocopying, recording or otherwise transmitted without written permission from the publisher. You must not circulate this book in any format.

TABLE OF CONTENTS

A Christmas Carol

A Christmas Carol	5
Background	11
December 1	13
December 2	18
December 3	26
December 4	31
December 5	37
December 6	43
December 7	51
December 8	58
December 9	65
December 10	71
December 11	77
December 12	86
December 13	92
December 14	100
December 15	108
December 16	114

December 17	120
December 18	126
December 19	132
December 20	139
December 21	147
December 22	154
December 23	162
December 24	168
Extension activities	176

The Life of Our Lord

Foreword	179
December 1	181
December 2	186
December 3	189
December 4	193
December 5	197
December 6	200
December 7	203
December 8	207
December 9	211

December 10	215
December 11	219
December 12	223
December 13	227
December 14	231
December 15	235
December 16	239
December 17	242
December 18	246
December 19	249
December 20	253
December 21	256
December 22	259
December 23	262
December 24	265
Extension Activities	270
What's Next?	272

A Christmas Carol

Special 24-Day Advent Reader

Charles Dickens

Background

During Dickens' lifetime, Christmas was not widely celebrated as it is today. It is in part due to the popularity of A Christmas Carol that the familiar themes in A Christmas Carol became a part of our culture today.

Charles Dickens wrote The Life of Our Lord for his children, and read it to them every year. He did not want it published during his lifetime or that of his children, so it wasn't until sixty-four years after his death that it was finally published.

The gap between rich and poor in England was huge. The poor were very poor, and conditions in London streets were filthy, with no idea of modern hygiene. Dickens had experienced poverty himself. With his father locked in debtors' prison, he was forced to work in a factory to help support his family.

~ ~ ~

In this Workman Family Classics edition of A Christmas Carol and The Life of Our Lord, spellings have been standardized to modern American and some punctuation and capitalization have been cleaned up. Dickens' use of commas was different from our modern usage, and for the more part, I have left them alone. In The Life of Our Lord, Dickens' use of commas and capitalization in the original manuscript was unusual, and for the more part, I have left them alone to keep it true to Dickens' handwritten copy. No attempt has been made to modernize or dumb down the original language. Footnotes have been included to explain archaic words and literary references.

These two books have each been formatted with a reading for every day in Advent, the days in December before Christmas so that you may enjoy short reading with your family (or on your own) in the days leading up to Christmas.

Enjoy your read!

P.D. Workman

December 1

MARLEY WAS DEAD, TO begin with. There is no doubt whatever about that. The register of his burial was signed by the clergyman, the clerk, the undertaker, and the chief mourner. Scrooge signed it. And Scrooge's name was good upon 'Change[1] for anything he chose to put his hand to. Old Marley was as dead as a door-nail.

Mind! I don't mean to say that I know, of my own knowledge, what there is particularly dead about a door-nail. I might have been inclined, myself, to regard a coffin-nail as the deadest piece of ironmongery in the trade. But the wisdom of our ancestors is in the simile; and my unhallowed hands shall not disturb it, or the

---

[1] Stock Exchange. Scrooge had good credit.

Country's done for. You will, therefore, permit me to repeat, emphatically, that Marley was as dead as a door-nail.

Scrooge knew he was dead? Of course he did. How could it be otherwise? Scrooge and he were partners for I don't know how many years. Scrooge was his sole executor, his sole administrator, his sole assign, his sole residuary legatee, his sole friend, and sole mourner. And even Scrooge was not so dreadfully cut up by the sad event, but that he was an excellent man of business on the very day of the funeral, and solemnized it with an undoubted bargain.

The mention of Marley's funeral brings me back to the point I started from. There is no doubt that Marley was dead. This must be distinctly understood, or nothing wonderful can come of the story I am going to relate. If we were not perfectly convinced that Hamlet's Father died before the play began, there would be nothing more remarkable in his taking a stroll at night, in an easterly wind, upon his own ramparts, than there would be in any other middle-aged gentleman rashly turning out after dark in a breezy spot—say St. Paul's Churchyard, for instance—literally to astonish his son's weak mind.

Scrooge never painted out Old Marley's name. There it stood, years afterward, above the warehouse door: Scrooge and Marley. The firm was known as Scrooge and Marley. Sometimes people new to the business called Scrooge Scrooge, and sometimes Marley, but he answered to both names. It was all the same to him.

Oh! But he was a tight-fisted hand at the grindstone, Scrooge! A squeezing, wrenching, grasping, scraping, clutching, covetous, old sinner! Hard and sharp as flint, from which no steel had ever struck out generous fire; secret, and self-contained, and solitary as an oyster. The cold within him froze his old features, nipped his pointed nose, shriveled his cheek, stiffened his gait; made his eyes red, his thin lips blue; and spoke out shrewdly in his grating voice. A frosty rime was on his head, and on his eyebrows, and his wiry chin. He carried his own low temperature always about with him; he iced his office in the dog-days; and didn't thaw it one degree at Christmas.

External heat and cold had little influence on Scrooge. No warmth could warm, no wintry weather chill him. No wind that blew was bitterer than he, no falling snow was more intent upon its purpose, no pelting rain less open to entreaty. Foul weather didn't know where to have him. The heaviest rain, and snow, and hail, and sleet could boast of the

A CHRISTMAS CAROL

advantage over him in only one respect. They often "came down" handsomely and Scrooge never did.

Nobody ever stopped him in the street to say, with gladsome looks, "My dear Scrooge, how are you? When will you come to see me?" No beggars implored him to bestow a trifle, no children asked him what it was o'clock, no man or woman ever once in all his life inquired the way to such and such a place, of Scrooge. Even the blind men's dogs appeared to know him; and, when they saw him coming on, would tug their owners into doorways and up courts; and then would wag their tails as though they said, "No eye at all is better than an evil eye, dark master!"

But what did Scrooge care? It was the very thing he liked. To edge his way along the crowded paths of life, warning all human sympathy to keep its distance, was what the knowing ones call "nuts"[1] to Scrooge.

Once upon a time—of all the good days in the year, on Christmas Eve—old Scrooge sat busy in his counting house. It was cold, bleak, biting weather: foggy withal: and he could hear the people in the court outside go wheezing up and down, beating their hands upon their

---

[1] a pleasure

breasts, and stamping their feet upon the pavement stones to warm them. The City clocks had only just gone three, but it was quite dark already—it had not been light all day—and candles were flaring in the windows of the neighboring offices, like ruddy smears upon the palpable brown air. The fog came pouring in at every chink and keyhole, and was so dense without, that, although the court was of the narrowest, the houses opposite were mere phantoms. To see the dingy cloud come drooping down, obscuring everything, one might have thought that nature lived hard by and was brewing on a large scale.

Let all bitterness, and wrath, and anger, and clamor, and evil speaking, be put away from you, with all malice (Ephesians 4:31)

Discussion Question:
Was Scrooge a happy man?

December 2

THE DOOR OF SCROOGE'S counting house was open, that he might keep his eye upon his clerk, who in a dismal little cell beyond, a sort of tank, was copying letters. Scrooge had a very small fire, but the clerk's fire was so very much smaller that it looked like one coal. But he couldn't replenish it, for Scrooge kept the coal-box in his own room; and so surely as the clerk came in with the shovel, the master predicted that it would be necessary for them to part. Wherefore the clerk put on his white comforter, and tried to warm himself at the candle; in which effort, not being a man of strong imagination, he failed.

"A merry Christmas, uncle! God save you!" cried a cheerful voice. It was the voice of Scrooge's nephew, who came upon him so quickly that this was the first intimation he had of his approach.

"Bah!" said Scrooge. "Humbug!"

He had so heated himself with rapid walking in the fog and frost, this nephew of Scrooge's, that he was all in a glow; his face was ruddy and handsome; his eyes sparkled, and his breath smoked again.

"Christmas a humbug, uncle!" said Scrooge's nephew. "You don't mean that, I am sure?"

"I do," said Scrooge. "Merry Christmas! What right have you to be merry? What reason have you to be merry? You're poor enough."

"Come, then," returned the nephew gaily. "What right have you to be dismal? What reason have you to be morose? You're rich enough."

Scrooge, having no better answer ready on the spur of the moment, said, "Bah!" again; and followed it up with "Humbug!"

"Don't be cross, uncle!" said the nephew.

"What else can I be," returned the uncle, "when I live in such a world of fools as this? Merry Christmas! Out upon merry Christmas! What's Christmastime to you but a time for paying bills without money; a time for finding yourself a year older, and not an hour richer; a time for balancing your books, and having every item in 'em through a round dozen of months presented dead against you? If I could work my will," said Scrooge indignantly, "every idiot who goes about with 'Merry Christmas' on his lips should be boiled with his own pudding, and buried with a stake of holly through his heart. He should!"

"Uncle!" pleaded the nephew.

"Nephew!" returned the uncle sternly. "Keep Christmas in your own way, and let me keep it in mine."

"Keep it!" repeated Scrooge's nephew. "But you don't keep it."

"Let me leave it alone, then," said Scrooge. "Much good may it do you! Much good it has ever done you!"

"There are many things from which I might have derived good, by which I have not profited, I dare say," returned the nephew; "Christmas among the rest. But I am sure I have always thought of Christmastime, when it has come round—apart from the veneration due to its sacred name and origin, if anything belonging to it can be apart from that—as a good time; a kind, forgiving, charitable, pleasant time; the only time I know of, in the long calendar of the year, when men and women seem by one consent to open their shut-up hearts freely, and to think of people below them as if they really were fellow-passengers to the grave, and not another race of creatures bound on other journeys. And therefore, uncle, though it has never put a scrap of gold or silver in my pocket, I believe that it has done me good, and will do me good; and I say, God bless it!"

The clerk in the tank involuntarily applauded. Becoming immediately sensible of the impropriety, he poked the fire, and extinguished the last frail spark forever.

"Let me hear another sound from you," said Scrooge, "and you'll keep your Christmas by losing your situation! You're quite a powerful speaker, sir," he added, turning to his nephew. "I wonder you don't go into Parliament."

"Don't be angry, uncle. Come! Dine with us tomorrow."

Scrooge said that he would see him—Yes, indeed he did. He went the whole length of the expression, and said that he would see him in that extremity first.

"But why?" cried Scrooge's nephew. "Why?"

"Why did you get married?" said Scrooge.

"Because I fell in love."

"Because you fell in love!" growled Scrooge, as if that were the only one thing in the world more ridiculous than a merry Christmas. "Good afternoon!"

"Nay, uncle, but you never came to see me before that happened. Why give it as a reason for not coming now?"

"Good afternoon," said Scrooge.

"I want nothing from you; I ask nothing of you; why cannot we be friends?"

"Good afternoon!" said Scrooge.

"I am sorry, with all my heart, to find you so resolute. We have never had any quarrel to which I have been a party. But I have made the trial in homage to Christmas, and I'll keep my Christmas humor to the last. So A Merry Christmas, uncle!"

"Good afternoon," said Scrooge.

"And A Happy New Year!"

"Good afternoon!" said Scrooge.

His nephew left the room without an angry word, notwithstanding. He stopped at the outer door to bestow the greetings of the season on the clerk, who, cold as he was, was warmer than Scrooge; for he returned them cordially.

"There's another fellow," muttered Scrooge, who overheard him: "my clerk, with fifteen shillings a week, and a wife and family, talking about a merry Christmas. I'll retire to Bedlam."

This lunatic, in letting Scrooge's nephew out, had let two other people in. They were portly gentlemen, pleasant to behold, and now stood, with their hats off, in Scrooge's office. They had books and papers in their hands, and bowed to him.

"Scrooge and Marley's, I believe," said one of the gentlemen, referring to his list. "Have I the pleasure of addressing Mr. Scrooge, or Mr. Marley?"

"Mr. Marley has been dead these seven years," Scrooge replied. "He died seven years ago, this very night."

"We have no doubt his liberality is well represented by his surviving partner," said the gentleman, presenting his credentials.

It certainly was; for they had been two kindred spirits. At the ominous word "liberality" Scrooge frowned, and shook his head, and handed the credentials back.

"At this festive season of the year, Mr. Scrooge," said the gentleman, taking up a pen, "it is more than usually desirable that we should make some slight provision for the poor and destitute, who suffer greatly at the present time. Many thousands are in want of common necessaries; hundreds of thousands are in want of common comforts, sir."

"Are there no prisons?" asked Scrooge.

"Plenty of prisons," said the gentleman, laying down the pen again.

"And the Union workhouses?" demanded Scrooge. "Are they still in operation?"

"They are. Still," returned the gentleman, "I wish I could say they were not."

A CHRISTMAS CAROL

"The Treadmill[1] and the Poor Law are in full vigor, then?" said Scrooge.

"Both very busy, sir."

"Oh! I was afraid, from what you said at first, that something had occurred to stop them in their useful course," said Scrooge. "I am very glad to hear it."

"Under the impression that they scarcely furnish Christian cheer of mind or body to the multitude," returned the gentleman, "a few of us are endeavoring to raise a fund to buy the Poor some meat and drink, and means of warmth. We choose this time, because it is a time, of all others, when Want is keenly felt, and Abundance rejoices. What shall I put you down for?"

"Nothing!" Scrooge replied.

"You wish to be anonymous?"

"I wish to be left alone," said Scrooge. "Since you ask me what I wish, gentlemen, that is my answer. I don't make merry myself at Christmas, and I can't afford to make idle people merry. I help to support the establishments I have mentioned—they cost enough; and those who are badly off must go there."

---

[1] a machine designed to power a mill with manual labor

"Many can't go there; and many would rather die."

"If they would rather die," said Scrooge, "they had better do it, and decrease the surplus population. Besides—excuse me—I don't know that."

"But you might know it," observed the gentleman.

"It's not my business," Scrooge returned. "It's enough for a man to understand his own business, and not to interfere with other people's. Mine occupies me constantly. Good afternoon, gentlemen!"

Seeing clearly that it would be useless to pursue their point, the gentlemen withdrew. Scrooge resumed his labors with an improved opinion of himself, and in a more facetious temper[1] than was usual with him.

And above all things have fervent charity among yourselves: for charity shall cover the multitude of sins. (1 Peter 4:8)

Discussion question:
How does the way that Scrooge's society dealt with the poor and destitute different from the way we deal with the indigent and homeless today?

---

[1] joking mood

December 3

MEANWHILE THE FOG AND darkness thickened so, that people ran about with flaring links,[1] proffering their services to go before horses in carriages, and conduct them on their way. The ancient tower of a church, whose gruff old bell was always peeping slyly down at Scrooge out of a Gothic window in the wall, became invisible, and struck the hours and quarters in the clouds, with tremulous vibrations afterward, as if its teeth were chattering in its frozen head up there. The cold became intense. In the main street, at the corner of the court, some laborers were repairing the gas pipes, and had lighted a great fire in a brazier, round which a party of ragged men and boys were gathered: warming their hands and winking their eyes before the blaze in rapture. The water-plug being left in

---

[1] torches

solitude, its overflowings suddenly congealed, and turned to misanthropic ice. The brightness of the shops, where holly sprigs and berries crackled in the lamp heat of the windows, made pale faces ruddy as they passed. Poulterers' and grocers' trades became a splendid joke: a glorious pageant, with which it was next to impossible to believe that such dull principles as bargain and sale had anything to do. The Lord Mayor, in the stronghold of the mighty Mansion House, gave orders to his fifty cooks and butlers to keep Christmas as a Lord Mayor's household should; and even the little tailor, whom he had fined five shillings on the previous Monday for being drunk and bloodthirsty in the streets, stirred up tomorrow's pudding in his garret, while his lean wife and the baby sallied out to buy the beef.

Foggier yet, and colder! Piercing, searching, biting cold. If the good St. Dunstan had but nipped the Evil Spirit's nose with a touch of such weather as that, instead of using his familiar weapons, then indeed he would have roared to lusty purpose.[1] The owner of one

---

[1] St Dunstan, as the story goes,
Once pull'd the devil by the nose
With red-hot tongs, which made him roar,
That he was heard three miles or more.

A CHRISTMAS CAROL

scant young nose, gnawed and mumbled by the hungry cold as bones are gnawed by dogs, stooped down at Scrooge's keyhole to regale him with a Christmas carol; but, at the first sound of "God bless you, merry gentleman, May nothing you dismay!" Scrooge seized the ruler with such energy of action, that the singer fled in terror, leaving the keyhole to the fog, and even more congenial frost.

At length the hour of shutting up the counting house arrived.

With an ill-will Scrooge dismounted from his stool, and tacitly admitted the fact to the expectant clerk in the tank, who instantly snuffed his candle out, and put on his hat.

"You'll want all day tomorrow, I suppose?" said Scrooge.

"If quite convenient, sir."

"It's not convenient," said Scrooge, "and it's not fair. If I was to stop half-a-crown for it, you'd think yourself ill used, I'll be bound?"

The clerk smiled faintly.

"And yet," said Scrooge, "you don't think me ill used when I pay a day's wages for no work."

The clerk observed that it was only once a year.

(folk rhyme)

CHARLES DICKENS

"A poor excuse for picking a man's pocket every twenty-fifth of December!" said Scrooge, buttoning his great-coat to the chin. "But I suppose you must have the whole day. Be here all the earlier next morning."

The clerk promised that he would; and Scrooge walked out with a growl. The office was closed in a twinkling, and the clerk, with the long ends of his white comforter dangling below his waist (for he boasted no great-coat), went down a slide on Cornhill, at the end of a lane of boys, twenty times, in honor of its being Christmas Eve, and then ran home to Camden Town as hard as he could pelt, to play at blind man's buff.

Scrooge took his melancholy dinner in his usual melancholy tavern; and having read all the newspapers, and beguiled the rest of the evening with his banker's book, went home to bed. He lived in chambers which had once belonged to his deceased partner. They were a gloomy suite of rooms, in a lowering pile of building up a yard, where it had so little business to be, that one could scarcely help fancying it must have run there when it was a young house, playing at hide-and-seek with other houses, and have forgotten the way out again. It was old enough now, and dreary enough; for nobody lived in it but Scrooge, the

A CHRISTMAS CAROL

other rooms being all let out as offices. The yard was so dark that even Scrooge, who knew its every stone, was fain to grope with his hands. The fog and frost so hung about the black old gateway of the house, that it seemed as if the Genius of the Weather sat in mournful meditation on the threshold.

The laborer is worthy of his hire (Luke 10:7)

Discussion Question:
Scrooge goes home in misery, and Cratchit, the clerk, in great cheer. Why?

December 4

Now, it is a fact that there was nothing at all particular about the knocker on the door, except that it was very large. It is also a fact that Scrooge had seen it, night and morning, during his whole residence in that place; also that Scrooge had as little of what is called fancy about him as any man in the City of London, even including—which is a bold word—the corporation, aldermen, and livery. Let it also be borne in mind that Scrooge had not bestowed one thought on Marley since his last mention of his seven-years'-dead partner that afternoon. And then let any man explain to me, if he can, how it happened that Scrooge, having his key in the lock of the door, saw in the knocker, without its undergoing any intermediate process of change—not a knocker, but Marley's face.

A CHRISTMAS CAROL

Marley's face. It was not in impenetrable shadow, as the other objects in the yard were, but had a dismal light about it, like a bad lobster in a dark cellar.[1] It was not angry or ferocious, but looked at Scrooge as Marley used to look: with ghostly spectacles turned up on its ghostly forehead. The hair was curiously stirred, as if by breath of hot air; and, though the eyes were wide open, they were perfectly motionless. That, and its livid color, made it horrible; but its horror seemed to be in spite of the face, and beyond its control, rather than a part of its own expression.

As Scrooge looked fixedly at this phenomenon, it was a knocker again.

To say that he was not startled, or that his blood was not conscious of a terrible sensation to which it had been a stranger from infancy, would be untrue. But he put his hand upon the key he had relinquished, turned it sturdily, walked in, and lighted his candle.

He did pause, with a moment's irresolution, before he shut the door; and he did look cautiously behind it first, as if he half expected to be terrified with the sight of Marley's pigtail sticking out into the hall. But there was nothing

---

[1] Supposedly, the bacteria in bad seafood would make it phosphorescent.

on the back of the door, except the screws and nuts that held the knocker on, so he said, "Pooh, pooh!" and closed it with a bang.

The sound resounded through the house like thunder. Every room above, and every cask in the wine merchant's cellars below, appeared to have a separate peal of echoes of its own. Scrooge was not a man to be frightened by echoes. He fastened the door, and walked across the hall, and up the stairs: slowly, too: trimming his candle as he went.

You may talk vaguely about driving a coach and six up a good old flight of stairs, or through a bad young Act of Parliament; but I mean to say you might have got a hearse up that staircase, and taken it broadwise, with the splinter-bar towards the wall, and the door towards the balustrades: and done it easy. There was plenty of width for that, and room to spare; which is perhaps the reason why Scrooge thought he saw a locomotive hearse going on before him in the gloom. Half a dozen gas lamps out of the street wouldn't have lighted the entry too well, so you may suppose that it was pretty dark with Scrooge's dip.

Up Scrooge went, not caring a button for that. Darkness is cheap, and Scrooge liked it. But, before he shut his heavy door, he walked through his rooms to see that all was right. He had just enough recollection of the face to desire to do that.

Sitting room, bedroom, lumber room.[1] All as they should be. Nobody under the table, nobody under the sofa; a small fire in the grate; spoon and basin ready; and the little saucepan of gruel (Scrooge had a cold in his head) upon the hob. Nobody under the bed; nobody in the closet; nobody in his dressing gown, which was hanging up in a suspicious attitude against the wall. Lumber room as usual. Old fire-guard, old shoes, two fish baskets, washing-stand on three legs, and a poker.

Quite satisfied, he closed his door, and locked himself in; double locked himself in, which was not his custom. Thus secured against surprise, he took off his cravat; put on his dressing gown and slippers, and his nightcap; and sat down before the fire to take his gruel.

It was a very low fire indeed; nothing on such a bitter night. He was obliged to sit close to it, and brood over it, before he could extract the least sensation of warmth from such a handful of fuel. The fireplace was an old one, built by some Dutch merchant long ago, and paved all round with quaint Dutch tiles, designed to illustrate the Scriptures. There were

---

[1] A room to store unused furniture.

Cains and Abels, Pharaoh's daughters, Queens of Sheba, Angelic messengers descending through the air on clouds like feather beds, Abrahams, Belshazzars, Apostles putting off to sea in butter-boats, hundreds of figures to attract his thoughts; and yet that face of Marley, seven years dead, came like the ancient Prophet's rod, and swallowed up the whole.[1] If each smooth tile had been a blank at first, with power to shape some picture on its surface from the disjointed fragments of his thoughts, there would have been a copy of old Marley's head on every one.

"Humbug!" said Scrooge; and walked across the room.

After several turns he sat down again. As he threw his head back in the chair, his glance happened to rest upon a bell, a disused bell, that hung in the room, and communicated, for some purpose now forgotten, with a chamber in the highest story of the building. It was with great astonishment, and with a strange, inexplicable dread, that, as he looked, he saw this bell begin to swing. It swung so softly in the outset that it scarcely made a sound; but

---

[1] Moses' staff miraculously turned into a snake, and swallowed the snakes of the Pharaoh's magicians.

A CHRISTMAS CAROL

soon it rang out loudly, and so did every bell in the house.

Behold, I send my messenger before thy face, which shall prepare thy way before thee. (Luke 7:27)

Discussion Question:
Why did Scrooge eat in the dark?

December 5

THIS MIGHT HAVE LASTED half a minute, or a minute, but it seemed an hour. The bells ceased, as they had begun, together. They were succeeded by a clanking noise, deep down below, as if some person were dragging a heavy chain over the casks in the wine merchant's cellar. Scrooge then remembered to have heard that ghosts in haunted houses were described as dragging chains.

The cellar door flew open with a booming sound, and then he heard the noise much louder on the floors below; then coming up the stairs; then coming straight towards his door.

"It's humbug still!" said Scrooge. "I won't believe it."

His color changed, though, when, without a pause, it came on through the heavy door, and passed into the room before his eyes. Upon its coming in, the dying flame leaped up, as though it cried, "I know him! Marley's Ghost!" and fell again.

The same face: the very same. Marley in his pigtail, usual waistcoat, tights, and boots; the tassels on the latter bristling, like his pigtail, and his coat-skirts, and the hair upon his head. The chain he drew was clasped about his middle. It was long, and wound about him like a tail; and it was made (for Scrooge observed it closely) of cash-boxes, keys, padlocks, ledgers, deeds, and heavy purses wrought in steel. His body was transparent; so that Scrooge, observing him, and looking through his waistcoat, could see the two buttons on his coat behind.

Scrooge had often heard it said that Marley had no bowels, but he had never believed it until now.

No, nor did he believe it even now. Though he looked the phantom through and through, and saw it standing before him; though he felt the chilling influence of its death-cold eyes; and marked the very texture of the folded kerchief bound about its head and chin, which wrapper he had not observed before; he was still incredulous, and fought against his senses.

"How now!" said Scrooge, caustic and cold as ever. "What do you want with me?"

"Much!"—Marley's voice, no doubt about it.

"Who are you?"

"Ask me who I was."

"Who were you, then?" said Scrooge, raising his voice. "You're particular, for a shade." He was going to say "to a shade," but substituted this, as more appropriate.[1]

"In life I was your partner, Jacob Marley."

"Can you—can you sit down?" asked Scrooge, looking doubtfully at him.

"I can."

"Do it, then."

Scrooge asked the question, because he didn't know whether a ghost so transparent might find himself in a condition to take a chair; and felt that, in the event of its being impossible, it might involve the necessity of an embarrassing explanation. But the Ghost sat down on the opposite side of the fireplace, as if he were quite used to it.

"You don't believe in me," observed the Ghost.

"I don't," said Scrooge.

"What evidence would you have of my reality beyond that of your own senses?"

---

[1] you're particular to a shade - you are nitpicking

you're particular for a shade - for a ghost, you're opinionated

"I don't know," said Scrooge.

"Why do you doubt your senses?"

"Because," said Scrooge, "a little thing affects them. A slight disorder of the stomach makes them cheats. You may be an undigested bit of beef, a blot of mustard, a crumb of cheese, a fragment of an underdone potato. There's more of gravy than of grave about you, whatever you are!"

Scrooge was not much in the habit of cracking jokes, nor did he feel in his heart by any means waggish then. The truth is, that he tried to be smart, as a means of distracting his own attention, and keeping down his terror; for the specter's voice disturbed the very marrow in his bones.

To sit staring at those fixed glazed eyes in silence, for a moment, would play, Scrooge felt, the very deuce with him. There was something very awful, too, in the specter's being provided with an infernal atmosphere of his own. Scrooge could not feel it himself, but this was clearly the case; for though the Ghost sat perfectly motionless, its hair, and skirts, and tassels were still agitated as by the hot vapor from an oven.

"You see this toothpick?" said Scrooge, returning quickly to the charge, for the reason just assigned; and wishing, though it were only for a second, to divert the vision's stony gaze from himself.

"I do," replied the Ghost.

"You are not looking at it," said Scrooge.

"But I see it," said the Ghost, "notwithstanding."

"Well!" returned Scrooge, "I have but to swallow this, and be for the rest of my days persecuted by a legion of goblins, all of my own creation. Humbug, I tell you; humbug!"

At this the spirit raised a frightful cry, and shook its chain with such a dismal and appalling noise, that Scrooge held on tight to his chair, to save himself from falling in a swoon. But how much greater was his horror when the phantom, taking off the bandage round his head, as if it were too warm to wear indoors, its lower jaw dropped down upon its breast!

Scrooge fell upon his knees, and clasped his hands before his face.

"Mercy!" he said. "Dreadful apparition, why do you trouble me?"

"Man of the worldly mind!" replied the Ghost. "Do you believe in me or not?"

"I do," said Scrooge. "I must. But why do spirits walk the earth, and why do they come to me?"

"It is required of every man," the Ghost returned, "that the spirit within him should walk abroad among his fellowmen, and travel far and wide; and, if that spirit goes not forth in life, it is condemned to do so after death. It is doomed to wander through the world—oh, woe is me!—And witness what it cannot share, but might have shared on earth, and turned to happiness!"

There is no man that hath power over the spirit to retain the spirit; neither hath he power in the day of death (Ecclesiastes 8:8)

Discussion Question:
Why won't Scrooge believe in a spirit even when he sees one in front of him?

December 6

AGAIN THE SPECTER RAISED a cry, and shook its chain and wrung its shadowy hands.

"You are fettered," said Scrooge, trembling. "Tell me why?"

"I wear the chain I forged in life," replied the Ghost. "I made it link by link, and yard by yard; I girded it on of my own free will, and of my own free will I wore it. Is its pattern strange to you?"

Scrooge trembled more and more.

"Or would you know," pursued the Ghost, "the weight and length of the strong coil you bear yourself? It was full as heavy and as long as this, seven Christmas Eves ago. You have labored on it since. It is a ponderous chain!"

Scrooge glanced about him on the floor, in the expectation of finding himself surrounded by some fifty or sixty fathoms of iron cable, but he could see nothing.

"Jacob!" he said imploringly. "Old Jacob Marley, tell me more! Speak comfort to me, Jacob!"

"I have none to give," the Ghost replied. "It comes from other regions, Ebenezer Scrooge, and is conveyed by other ministers, to other kinds of men. Nor can I tell you what I would. A very little more is all permitted to me. I cannot rest, I cannot stay, I cannot linger anywhere. My spirit never walked beyond our counting house—mark me;—in life my spirit never roved beyond the narrow limits of our money-changing hole; and weary journeys lie before me!"

It was a habit with Scrooge, whenever he became thoughtful, to put his hands in his breeches pockets. Pondering on what the Ghost had said, he did so now, but without lifting up his eyes, or getting off his knees.

"You must have been very slow about it, Jacob," Scrooge observed in a businesslike manner, though with humility and deference.

"Slow!" the Ghost repeated.

"Seven years dead," mused Scrooge. "And traveling all the time?"

"The whole time," said the Ghost. "No rest, no peace. Incessant torture of remorse."

"You travel fast?" said Scrooge.

"On the wings of the wind," replied the Ghost.

"You might have got over a great quantity of ground in seven years," said Scrooge.

The Ghost, on hearing this, set up another cry, and clanked its chain so hideously in the dead silence of the night, that the Ward would have been justified in indicting it for a nuisance.

"Oh! Captive, bound, and double-ironed," cried the phantom, "not to know that ages of incessant labor, by immortal creatures, for this earth must pass into eternity before the good of which it is susceptible is all developed! Not to know that any Christian spirit working kindly in its little sphere, whatever it may be, will find its mortal life too short for its vast means of usefulness! Not to know that no space of regret can make amends for one life's opportunities misused! Yet such was I! Oh, such was I!"

"But you were always a good man of business, Jacob," faltered Scrooge, who now began to apply this to himself.

"Business!" cried the Ghost, wringing its hands again. "Mankind was my business. The common welfare was my business; charity, mercy, forbearance, and benevolence were, all, my business. The dealings of my trade were but a drop of water in the comprehensive ocean of my business!"

A CHRISTMAS CAROL

It held up its chain at arm's length, as if that were the cause of all its unavailing grief, and flung it heavily upon the ground again.

"At this time of the rolling year," the specter said, "I suffer most. Why did I walk through crowds of fellow beings with my eyes turned down, and never raise them to that blessed Star which led the Wise Men to a poor abode? Were there no poor homes to which its light would have conducted me?"

Scrooge was very much dismayed to hear the specter going on at this rate, and began to quake exceedingly.

"Hear me!" cried the Ghost. "My time is nearly gone."

"I will," said Scrooge. "But don't be hard upon me! Don't be flowery, Jacob! Pray!"

"How it is that I appear before you in a shape that you can see, I may not tell. I have sat invisible beside you many and many a day."

It was not an agreeable idea. Scrooge shivered, and wiped the perspiration from his brow.

"That is no light part of my penance," pursued the Ghost. "I am here tonight to warn you that you have yet a chance and hope of escaping my fate. A chance and hope of my procuring, Ebenezer."

"You were always a good friend to me," said Scrooge. "Thankee!"

"You will be haunted," resumed the Ghost, "by Three Spirits."

Scrooge's countenance fell almost as low as the Ghost's had done.

"Is that the chance and hope you mentioned, Jacob?" he demanded in a faltering voice.

"It is."

"I—I think I'd rather not," said Scrooge.

"Without their visits," said the Ghost, "you cannot hope to shun the path I tread. Expect the first tomorrow when the bell tolls One."

"Couldn't I take 'em all at once, and have it over, Jacob?" hinted Scrooge.

"Expect the second on the next night at the same hour. The third, upon the next night when the last stroke of Twelve has ceased to vibrate. Look to see me no more; and look that, for your own sake, you remember what has passed between us!"

When it had said these words, the specter took its wrapper from the table, and bound it round its head as before. Scrooge knew this by the smart sound its teeth made when the jaws were brought together by the bandage. He ventured to raise his eyes again, and found his supernatural visitor confronting him in an erect attitude, with its chain wound over and about its arm.

The apparition walked backward from him; and, at every step it took, the window raised itself a little, so that, when the specter reached it, it was wide open. It beckoned Scrooge to approach, which he did. When they were within two paces of each other, Marley's Ghost held up its hand, warning him to come no nearer. Scrooge stopped.

Not so much in obedience as in surprise and fear; for, on the raising of the hand, he became sensible of confused noises in the air; incoherent sounds of lamentation and regret; wailings inexpressibly sorrowful and self-accusatory. The specter, after listening for a moment, joined in the mournful dirge; and floated out upon the bleak, dark night.

Scrooge followed to the window: desperate in his curiosity. He looked out.

The air was filled with phantoms, wandering hither and thither in restless haste, and moaning as they went. Every one of them wore chains like Marley's Ghost; some few (they might be guilty governments) were linked together; none were free. Many had been personally known to Scrooge in their lives. He had been quite familiar with one old ghost in a white waistcoat, with a monstrous iron safe attached to its ankle, who cried piteously at being unable to assist a wretched woman with an infant, whom it saw below upon a doorstep. The misery with them all was, clearly, that they sought to interfere, for good, in human matters, and had lost the power forever.

Whether these creatures faded into mist, or mist enshrouded them, he could not tell. But they and their spirit voices faded together; and the night became as it had been when he walked home.

Scrooge closed the window, and examined the door by which the Ghost had entered. It was double locked, as he had locked it with his own hands, and the bolts were undisturbed. He tried to say "Humbug!" but stopped at the first syllable. And being, from the emotion he had undergone, or the fatigues of the day, or his glimpse of the Invisible World, or the dull conversation of the Ghost, or the lateness of the hour, much in need of repose, went straight to bed without undressing, and fell asleep upon the instant.

A new commandment I give unto you, That ye love one another; as I have loved you, that ye also love one another.
(John 13:34)

A CHRISTMAS CAROL

Discussion Question:
What is your business? Are you a good steward of your business?

December 7

HEN SCROOGE AWOKE IT was so dark, that, looking out of bed, he could scarcely distinguish the transparent window from the opaque walls of his chamber. He was endeavoring to pierce the darkness with his ferret eyes, when the chimes of a neighboring church struck the four quarters. So he listened for the hour.

To his great astonishment, the heavy bell went on from six to seven, and from seven to eight, and regularly up to twelve; then stopped. Twelve! It was past two when he went to bed. The clock was wrong. An icicle must have got into the works. Twelve!

He touched the spring of his repeater,[1] to correct this most preposterous clock. Its rapid little pulse beat twelve, and stopped.

---

[1] A pocketwatch that chimes the hours at the press of a button.

"Why, it isn't possible," said Scrooge, "that I can have slept through a whole day and far into another night. It isn't possible that anything has happened to the sun, and this is twelve at noon!"

The idea being an alarming one, he scrambled out of bed, and groped his way to the window. He was obliged to rub the frost off with the sleeve of his dressing gown before he could see anything; and could see very little then. All he could make out was, that it was still very foggy and extremely cold, and that there was no noise of people running to and fro, and making a great stir, as there unquestionably would have been if night had beaten off bright day, and taken possession of the world. This was a great relief, because "Three days after sight of this First of Exchange pay to Mr. Ebenezer Scrooge or his order," and so forth, would have become a mere United States security if there were no days to count by.[1]

Scrooge went to bed again, and thought, and thought, and thought it over and over, and could make nothing of it. The more he thought,

---

[1] If the sun had failed to rise, the notes due to Scrooge at the Stock Exchange would be worth nothing (as apparently United States securities were at the time.)

the more perplexed he was; and, the more he endeavored not to think, the more he thought.

Marley's Ghost bothered him exceedingly. Every time he resolved within himself, after mature inquiry, that it was all a dream, his mind flew back again, like a strong spring released, to its first position, and presented the same problem to be worked all through, "Was it a dream or not?"

Scrooge lay in this state until the chime had gone three-quarters more, when he remembered, on a sudden, that the Ghost had warned him of a visitation when the bell tolled one. He resolved to lie awake until the hour was passed; and, considering that he could no more go to sleep than go to Heaven, this was, perhaps, the wisest resolution in his power.

The quarter was so long, that he was more than once convinced he must have sunk into a doze unconsciously, and missed the clock. At length it broke upon his listening ear.

"Ding, dong!"

"A quarter past," said Scrooge, counting.

"Ding, dong!"

"Half past," said Scrooge.

"Ding, dong!"

"A quarter to it," said Scrooge.

"Ding, dong!"

"The hour itself," said Scrooge triumphantly, "and nothing else!"

He spoke before the hour bell sounded, which it now did with a deep, dull, hollow, melancholy One. Light flashed up in the room upon the instant, and the curtains of his bed were drawn.

The curtains of his bed were drawn aside, I tell you, by a hand. Not the curtains at his feet, nor the curtains at his back, but those to which his face was addressed. The curtains of his bed were drawn aside; and Scrooge, starting up into a half-recumbent attitude, found himself face-to-face with the unearthly visitor who drew them: as close to it as I am now to you, and I am standing in the spirit at your elbow.

It was a strange figure—like a child: yet not so like a child as like an old man, viewed through some supernatural medium, which gave him the appearance of having receded from the view, and being diminished to a child's proportions. Its hair, which hung about its neck and down its back, was white, as if with age; and yet the face had not a wrinkle in it, and the tenderest bloom was on the skin. The arms were very long and muscular; the hands the same, as if its hold were of uncommon strength. Its legs and feet, most delicately formed, were, like those upper members, bare.

It wore a tunic of the purest white; and round its waist was bound a lustrous belt, the sheen of which was beautiful. It held a branch of fresh green holly in its hand: and, in singular contradiction of that wintry emblem, had its dress trimmed with summer flowers. But the strangest thing about it was, that from the crown of its head there sprung a bright clear jet of light, by which all this was visible; and which was doubtless the occasion of its using, in its duller moments, a great extinguisher for a cap, which it now held under its arm.

Even this, though, when Scrooge looked at it with increasing steadiness, was not its strangest quality. For, as its belt sparkled and glittered, now in one part and now in another, and what was light one instant at another time was dark, so the figure itself fluctuated in its distinctness: being now a thing with one arm, now with one leg, now with twenty legs, now a pair of legs without a head, now a head without a body: of which dissolving parts no outline would be visible in the dense gloom wherein they melted away. And, in the very wonder of this, it would be itself again; distinct and clear as ever.

"Are you the Spirit, sir, whose coming was foretold to me?" asked Scrooge.

"I am!"

A CHRISTMAS CAROL

The voice was soft and gentle. Singularly low, as if, instead of being so close beside him, it were at a distance.

"Who and what are you?" Scrooge demanded.

"I am the Ghost of Christmas Past."

"Long Past?" inquired Scrooge; observant of its dwarfish stature.

"No. Your past."

Perhaps Scrooge could not have told anybody why, if anybody could have asked him; but he had a special desire to see the Spirit in his cap; and begged him to be covered.

"What!" exclaimed the Ghost. "Would you so soon put out, with worldly hands, the light I give? Is it not enough that you are one of those whose passions made this cap, and force me through whole trains of years to wear it low upon my brow?"

Scrooge reverently disclaimed all intention to offend or any knowledge of having willfully "bonneted" the Spirit at any period of his life. He then made bold to inquire what business brought him there.

"Your welfare!" said the Ghost.

Scrooge expressed himself much obliged, but could not help thinking that a night of unbroken rest would have been more conducive to that end. The Spirit must have heard him thinking, for it said immediately:

"Your reclamation, then. Take heed!"

It put out its strong hand as it spoke, and clasped him gently by the arm.

"Rise! And walk with me!"

Ye do well that ye take heed, as unto a light that shineth in a dark place, until the day dawn (2 Peter 1:19)

Discussion Question:
How do we put the cap on Christmas spirit the rest of the year?

December 8

IT WOULD HAVE BEEN in vain for Scrooge to plead that the weather and the hour were not adapted to pedestrian purposes; that bed was warm, and the thermometer a long way below freezing; that he was clad but lightly in his slippers, dressing gown, and nightcap; and that he had a cold upon him at that time. The grasp, though gentle as a woman's hand, was not to be resisted. He rose: but, finding that the Spirit made towards the window, clasped its robe in supplication.

"I am a mortal," Scrooge remonstrated, "and liable to fall."

"Bear but a touch of my hand there," said the Spirit, laying it upon his heart, "and you shall be upheld in more than this!"

As the words were spoken, they passed through the wall, and stood upon an open country road, with fields on either hand. The city had entirely vanished. Not a vestige of it was to be seen. The darkness and the mist had vanished with it, for it was a clear, cold, winter day, with the snow upon the ground.

"Good Heaven!" said Scrooge, clasping his hands together as he looked about him. "I was bred in this place. I was a boy here!"

The Spirit gazed upon him mildly. Its gentle touch, though it had been light and instantaneous, appeared still present to the old man's sense of feeling. He was conscious of a thousand odors floating in the air, each one connected with a thousand thoughts, and hopes, and joys, and cares long, long forgotten!

"Your lip is trembling," said the Ghost. "And what is that upon your cheek?"

Scrooge muttered, with an unusual catching in his voice, that it was a pimple; and begged the Ghost to lead him where he would.

"You recollect the way?" inquired the Spirit.

"Remember it!" cried Scrooge with fervor; "I could walk it blindfold."

"Strange to have forgotten it for so many years!" observed the Ghost. "Let us go on."

They walked along the road, Scrooge recognizing every gate, and post, and tree, until a little market town appeared in the distance, with its bridge, its church, and winding river. Some shaggy ponies now were seen trotting towards them with boys upon their backs, who called to other boys in country gigs and carts, driven by farmers. All these boys were in great spirits, and shouted to each other, until the broad fields were so full of merry music, that the crisp air laughed to hear it.

"These are but shadows of the things that have been," said the Ghost. "They have no consciousness of us."

The jocund travelers came on; and as they came, Scrooge knew and named them every one. Why was he rejoiced beyond all bounds to see them? Why did his cold eye glisten, and his heart leap up as they went past? Why was he filled with gladness when he heard them give each other Merry Christmas, as they parted at crossroads and byways for their several homes? What was merry Christmas to Scrooge? Out upon merry Christmas! What good had it ever done to him?

"The school is not quite deserted," said the Ghost. "A solitary child, neglected by his friends, is left there still."

Scrooge said he knew it. And he sobbed.

They left the high road by a well-remembered lane, and soon approached a mansion of dull red brick, with a little weather-cock surmounted cupola on the roof and a bell hanging in it. It was a large house, but one of broken fortunes: for the spacious offices were little used, their walls were damp and mossy, their windows broken, and their gates decayed. Fowls clucked and strutted in the stables; and the coach-houses and sheds were overrun with grass. Nor was it more retentive of its ancient state within; for, entering the dreary hall, and glancing through the open doors of many rooms, they found them poorly furnished, cold, and vast. There was an earthly savor in the air, a chilly bareness in the place, which associated itself somehow with too much getting up by candle-light, and not too much to eat.

They went, the Ghost and Scrooge, across the hall, to a door at the back of the house. It opened before them, and disclosed a long, bare, melancholy room, made barer still by lines of plain deal forms and desks. At one of these a lonely boy was reading near a feeble fire; and Scrooge sat down upon a form, and wept to see his poor forgotten self as he had used to be.

Not a latent echo in the house, not a squeak and scuffle from the mice behind the paneling, not a drip from the half-thawed water-spout in the dull yard behind, not a sigh among the leafless boughs of one despondent poplar, not the idle swinging of an empty storehouse door, no, not a clicking in the fire, but fell upon the

A CHRISTMAS CAROL

heart of Scrooge with softening influence, and gave a freer passage to his tears.

The Spirit touched him on the arm, and pointed to his younger self, intent upon his reading. Suddenly a man in foreign garments: wonderfully real and distinct to look at: stood outside the window, with an axe stuck in his belt, and leading by the bridle an ass laden with wood.

"Why, it's Ali Baba!" Scrooge exclaimed in ecstasy. "It's dear old honest Ali Baba! Yes, yes, I know. One Christmastime when yonder solitary child was left here all alone, he did come, for the first time, just like that. Poor boy! And Valentine," said Scrooge, "and his wild brother, Orson; there they go! And what's his name, who was put down in his drawers, asleep, at the gate of Damascus; don't you see him? And the Sultan's Groom turned upside down by the Genii: there he is upon his head! Serve him right! I'm glad of it. What business had he to be married to the Princess?"

To hear Scrooge expending all the earnestness of his nature on such subjects, in a most extraordinary voice between laughing and crying; and to see his heightened and excited face; would have been a surprise to his business friends in the City, indeed.

"There's the Parrot!" cried Scrooge. "Green body and yellow tail, with a thing like a lettuce growing out of the top of his head; there he is! Poor Robin Crusoe he called him, when he came home again after sailing round the island. 'Poor Robin Crusoe, where have you been, Robin Crusoe?' The man thought he was dreaming, but he wasn't. It was the Parrot, you know. There goes Friday, running for his life to the little creek! Halloa! Hoop! Halloo!"

Then, with a rapidity of transition very foreign to his usual character, he said, in pity for his former self, "Poor boy!" and cried again.

"I wish," Scrooge muttered, putting his hand in his pocket, and looking about him, after drying his eyes with his cuff: "but it's too late now."

"What is the matter?" asked the Spirit.

"Nothing," said Scrooge. "Nothing. There was a boy singing a Christmas Carol at my door last night. I should like to have given him something: that's all."

The Ghost smiled thoughtfully, and waved its hand: saying, as it did so, "Let us see another Christmas!"

And above all things have fervent charity among yourselves: for charity shall cover the multitude of sins. (1 Peter 4:8)

A CHRISTMAS CAROL

Discussion Question:
What caused Scrooge's change of heart toward the boy singing a Christmas Carol?

December 9

SCROOGE'S FORMER SELF GREW larger at the words, and the room became a little darker and more dirty. The panels shrunk, the windows cracked; fragments of plaster fell out of the ceiling, and the naked laths were shown instead; but how all this was brought about Scrooge knew no more than you do. He only knew that it was quite correct: that everything had happened so; that there he was, alone again, when all the other boys had gone home for the jolly holidays.

He was not reading now, but walking up and down despairingly. Scrooge looked at the Ghost, and, with a mournful shaking of his head, glanced anxiously towards the door.

It opened; and a little girl, much younger than the boy, came darting in, and, putting her arms about his neck, and often kissing him, addressed him as her "dear, dear brother."

A CHRISTMAS CAROL

"I have come to bring you home, dear brother!" said the child, clapping her tiny hands, and bending down to laugh. "To bring you home, home, home!"

"Home, little Fan?" returned the boy.

"Yes!" said the child, brimful of glee. "Home for good and all. Home for ever and ever. Father is so much kinder than he used to be, that home's like Heaven! He spoke so gently to me one dear night when I was going to bed, that I was not afraid to ask him once more if you might come home; and he said Yes, you should; and sent me in a coach to bring you. And you're to be a man!" said the child, opening her eyes; "And are never to come back here; but first we're to be together all the Christmas long, and have the merriest time in all the world."

"You are quite a woman, little Fan!" exclaimed the boy.

She clapped her hands and laughed, and tried to touch his head; but, being too little, laughed again, and stood on tiptoe to embrace him. Then she began to drag him, in her childish eagerness, toward the door; and he, nothing loath to go, accompanied her.

A terrible voice in the hall cried, "Bring down Master Scrooge's box, there!" and in the hall appeared the schoolmaster himself, who glared on Master Scrooge with a ferocious condescension, and threw him into a dreadful state of mind by shaking hands with him. He then conveyed him and his sister into the veriest old well of a shivering best parlor that ever was seen, where the maps upon the wall, and the celestial and terrestrial globes in the windows, were waxy with cold. Here he produced a decanter of curiously light wine, and a block of curiously heavy cake, and administered installments of those dainties to the young people: at the same time sending out a meager servant to offer a glass of "something" to the postboy who answered that he thanked the gentleman, but, if it was the same tap as he had tasted before, he had rather not. Master Scrooge's trunk being by this time tied on to the top of the chaise, the children bade the schoolmaster good-bye right willingly; and, getting into it, drove gaily down the garden sweep; the quick wheels dashing the hoar frost and snow from off the dark leaves of the evergreens like spray.

"Always a delicate creature, whom a breath might have withered," said the Ghost. "But she had a large heart!"

"So she had," cried Scrooge. "You're right. I will not gainsay it, Spirit. God forbid!"

"She died a woman," said the Ghost, "and had, as I think, children."

"One child," Scrooge returned.

"True," said the Ghost. "Your nephew!"

Scrooge seemed uneasy in his mind; and answered briefly, "Yes."

Although they had but that moment left the school behind them, they were now in the busy thoroughfares of a city, where shadowy passengers passed and repassed; where shadowy carts and coaches battled for the way, and all the strife and tumult of a real city were. It was made plain enough, by the dressing of the shops, that here, too, it was Christmastime again; but it was evening, and the streets were lighted up.

The Ghost stopped at a certain warehouse door, and asked Scrooge if he knew it.

"Know it!" said Scrooge. "Was I apprenticed here?"

They went in. At sight of an old gentleman in a Welsh wig, sitting behind such a high desk, that if he had been two inches taller, he must have knocked his head against the ceiling, Scrooge cried in great excitement:

"Why, it's old Fezziwig! Bless his heart, it's Fezziwig alive again!"

Old Fezziwig laid down his pen, and looked up at the clock, which pointed to the hour of seven. He rubbed his hands; adjusted his capacious waistcoat; laughed all over himself, from his shoes to his organ of benevolence; and called out, in a comfortable, oily, rich, fat, jovial voice:

"Yo ho, there! Ebenezer! Dick!"

Scrooge's former self, now grown a young man, came briskly in, accompanied by his fellow-'prentice.

"Dick Wilkins, to be sure!" said Scrooge to the Ghost. "Bless me, yes. There he is. He was very much attached to me, was Dick. Poor Dick! Dear, dear!"

"Yo ho, my boys!" said Fezziwig. "No more work tonight. Christmas Eve, Dick. Christmas, Ebenezer! Let's have the shutters up," cried old Fezziwig with a sharp clap of his hands, "before a man can say Jack Robinson!"

You wouldn't believe how those two fellows went at it! They charged into the street with the shutters—one, two, three—had 'em up in their places—four, five, six—barred 'em and pinned 'em—seven, eight, nine—and came back before you could have got to twelve, panting like racehorses.

"Hilli-ho!" cried old Fezziwig, skipping down from the high desk with wonderful agility. "Clear away, my lads, and let's have lots of room here! Hilli-ho, Dick! Chirrup, Ebenezer!"

A CHRISTMAS CAROL

Clear away! There was nothing they wouldn't have cleared away, or couldn't have cleared away, with old Fezziwig looking on. It was done in a minute. Every movable was packed off, as if it were dismissed from public life forevermore; the floor was swept and watered, the lamps were trimmed, fuel was heaped upon the fire; and the warehouse was as snug, and warm, and dry, and bright a ballroom as you would desire to see upon a winter's night.

And we have known and believed the love that God hath to us. God is love; and he that dwelleth in love dwelleth in God, and God in him. (1 John 4:16)

Discussion Question:
What kind of a childhood did Scrooge have? How does this compare to modern times?

December 10

IN CAME A FIDDLER with a music book, and went up to the lofty desk, and made an orchestra of it, and tuned like fifty stomachaches. In came Mrs. Fezziwig, one vast substantial smile. In came the three Miss Fezziwigs, beaming and lovable. In came the six young followers whose hearts they broke. In came all the young men and women employed in the business.

In came the housemaid, with her cousin the baker. In came the cook, with her brother's particular friend the milkman. In came the boy from over the way, who was suspected of not having board[1] enough from his master; trying to hide himself behind the girl from next door but one, who was proved to have had her ears pulled by her mistress. In they all came, one after another; some shyly, some boldly, some

---

[1] food, meals

A CHRISTMAS CAROL

gracefully, some awkwardly, some pushing, some pulling; in they all came, anyhow and everyhow. Away they all went, twenty couple at once; hands half round and back again the other way; down the middle and up again; round and round in various stages of affectionate grouping; old top couple always turning up in the wrong place; new top couple starting off again as soon as they got there; all top couples at last, and not a bottom one to help them! When this result was brought about, old Fezziwig, clapping his hands to stop the dance, cried out, "Well done!" and the fiddler plunged his hot face into a pot of porter,[1] especially provided for that purpose. But, scorning rest upon his reappearance, he instantly began again, though there were no dancers yet, as if the other fiddler had been carried home, exhausted, on a shutter, and he were a bran-new man resolved to beat him out of sight, or perish.

There were more dances, and there were forfeits,[2] and more dances, and there was cake, and there was negus,[3] and there was a great piece of Cold Roast, and there was a great piece

---

[1] beer
[2] a party game
[3] wine

of Cold Boiled,[1] and there were mince pies, and plenty of beer. But the great effect of the evening came after the Roast and Boiled, when the fiddler (an artful dog, mind! The sort of man who knew his business better than you or I could have told it him!) struck up "Sir Roger de Coverley." Then old Fezziwig stood out to dance with Mrs. Fezziwig. Top couple, too; with a good stiff piece of work cut out for them; three or four and twenty pair of partners; people who were not to be trifled with; people who would dance, and had no notion of walking.

But if they had been twice as many—ah! Four times—old Fezziwig would have been a match for them, and so would Mrs. Fezziwig. As to her, she was worthy to be his partner in every sense of the term. If that's not high praise, tell me higher, and I'll use it. A positive light appeared to issue from Fezziwig's calves. They shone in every part of the dance like moons. You couldn't have predicted, at any given time, what would become of them next. And when old Fezziwig and Mrs. Fezziwig had gone all through the dance; advance and retire, both hands to your partner, bow and curtsy, corkscrew, thread-the-needle, and back again to

---

[1] beef or mutton "cold-cuts"

your place; Fezziwig "cut"—cut so deftly, that he appeared to wink with his legs, and came upon his feet again without a stagger.

When the clock struck eleven, this domestic ball broke up. Mr. and Mrs. Fezziwig took their stations, one on either side the door, and, shaking hands with every person individually as he or she went out, wished him or her a Merry Christmas. When everybody had retired but the two 'prentices, they did the same to them; and thus the cheerful voices died away, and the lads were left to their beds; which were under a counter in the back shop.

During the whole of this time Scrooge had acted like a man out of his wits. His heart and soul were in the scene, and with his former self. He corroborated everything, remembered everything, enjoyed everything, and underwent the strangest agitation. It was not until now, when the bright faces of his former self and Dick were turned from them, that he remembered the Ghost, and became conscious that it was looking full upon him, while the light upon its head burnt very clear.

"A small matter," said the Ghost, "to make these silly folks so full of gratitude."

"Small!" echoed Scrooge.

The Spirit signed to him to listen to the two apprentices, who were pouring out their hearts in praise of Fezziwig; and, when he had done so, said:

"Why! Is it not? He has spent but a few pounds of your mortal money: three or four, perhaps. Is that so much that he deserves this praise?"

"It isn't that," said Scrooge, heated by the remark, and speaking unconsciously like his former, not his latter self. "It isn't that, Spirit. He has the power to render us happy or unhappy; to make our service light or burdensome; a pleasure or a toil. Say that his power lies in words and looks; in things so slight and insignificant that it is impossible to add and count 'em up: what then? The happiness he gives is quite as great as if it cost a fortune."

He felt the Spirit's glance, and stopped.

"What is the matter?" asked the Ghost.

"Nothing particular," said Scrooge.

"Something, I think?" the Ghost insisted.

"No," said Scrooge, "no. I should like to be able to say a word or two to my clerk just now. That's all."

His former self turned down the lamps as he gave utterance to the wish; and Scrooge and the Ghost again stood side by side in the open air.

A CHRISTMAS CAROL

These things have I spoken unto you, that my joy might remain in you, and that your joy might be full. (John 15:11)

Discussion Question:

What did Scrooge want to say to his clerk? What can we do that will make those around us happy or unhappy?

December 11

"MY TIME GROWS SHORT," observed the Spirit. "Quick!"

This was not addressed to Scrooge, or to any one whom he could see, but it produced an immediate effect. For again Scrooge saw himself. He was older now; a man in the prime of life. His face had not the harsh and rigid lines of later years; but it had begun to wear the signs of care and avarice. There was an eager, greedy, restless motion in the eye, which showed the passion that had taken root, and where the shadow of the growing tree would fall.

He was not alone, but sat by the side of a fair young girl in a mourning dress: in whose eyes there were tears, which sparkled in the light that shone out of the Ghost of Christmas Past.

"It matters little," she said softly. "To you, very little. Another idol has displaced me; and, if it can cheer and comfort you in time to come as I would have tried to do, I have no just cause to grieve."

"What Idol has displaced you?" he rejoined.

"A golden one."

"This is the even-handed dealing of the world!" he said. "There is nothing on which it is so hard as poverty; and there is nothing it professes to condemn with such severity as the pursuit of wealth!"

"You fear the world too much," she answered gently. "All your other hopes have merged into the hope of being beyond the chance of its sordid reproach. I have seen your nobler aspirations fall off one by one, until the master passion, Gain, engrosses you. Have I not?"

"What then?" he retorted. "Even if I have grown so much wiser, what then? I am not changed towards you."

She shook her head.

"Am I?"

"Our contract is an old one. It was made when we were both poor, and content to be so, until, in good season, we could improve our worldly fortune by our patient industry. You are changed. When it was made you were another man."

"I was a boy," he said impatiently.

"Your own feeling tells you that you were not what you are," she returned. "I am. That which promised happiness when we were one in heart is fraught with misery now that we are two. How often and how keenly I have thought of this I will not say. It is enough that I have thought of it, and can release you."

"Have I ever sought release?"

"In words. No. Never."

"In what, then?"

"In a changed nature; in an altered spirit; in another atmosphere of life; another Hope as its great end. In everything that made my love of any worth or value in your sight. If this had never been between us," said the girl, looking mildly, but with steadiness, upon him, "tell me, would you seek me out and try to win me now? Ah, no!"

He seemed to yield to the justice of this supposition in spite of himself. But he said, with a struggle, "You think not."

"I would gladly think otherwise if I could," she answered. "Heaven knows! When I have learned a Truth like this, I know how strong and irresistible it must be. But if you were free today, tomorrow, yesterday, can even I believe that you would choose a dowerless girl—you who, in your very confidence with her, weigh everything by Gain: or, choosing her, if for a moment you were false enough to your one guiding principle to do so, do I not know that your repentance and regret would surely follow? I do; and I release you. With a full heart, for the love of him you once were."

He was about to speak; but, with her head turned from him, she resumed.

"You may—the memory of what is past half makes me hope you will—have pain in this. A very, very brief time, and you will dismiss the recollection of it gladly, as an unprofitable dream, from which it happened well that you awoke. May you be happy in the life you have chosen!"

She left him, and they parted.

"Spirit!" said Scrooge, "show me no more! Conduct me home. Why do you delight to torture me?"

"One shadow more!" exclaimed the Ghost.

"No more!" cried Scrooge. "No more! I don't wish to see it. Show me no more!"

But the relentless Ghost pinioned him in both his arms, and forced him to observe what happened next.

They were in another scene and place; a room, not very large or handsome, but full of comfort. Near to the winter fire sat a beautiful young girl, so like that last that Scrooge believed it was the same, until he saw her, now a comely matron, sitting opposite her daughter. The noise in this room was perfectly tumultuous, for there were more children there than Scrooge in his agitated state of mind could count; and, unlike the celebrated herd in the poem,[1] they were not forty children conducting themselves like one, but every child was conducting itself like forty. The consequences were uproarious beyond belief; but no one seemed to care; on the contrary, the mother and daughter laughed heartily, and enjoyed it very much; and the latter, soon beginning to mingle in the sports, got pillaged by the young brigands most ruthlessly. What would I not have given to be one of them! Though I never could have been so rude, no, no! I wouldn't for the wealth of all the world have crushed that braided hair, and torn it down; and, for the precious little shoe, I wouldn't have plucked it off, God bless my soul! To save my life. As to measuring her waist in sport, as they did, bold young brood, I couldn't have done it; I should have expected my arm to have grown round it for a punishment, and never come straight

---

[1] The cattle are grazing
Their heads never raising;
There are forty feeding like one!
(Wordsworth)

A CHRISTMAS CAROL

again. And yet I should have dearly liked, I own, to have touched her lips; to have questioned her, that she might have opened them; to have looked upon the lashes of her downcast eyes, and never raised a blush; to have let loose waves of hair, an inch of which would be a keepsake beyond price: in short, I should have liked, I do confess, to have had the lightest license of a child, and yet to have been man enough to know its value.

But now a knocking at the door was heard, and such a rush immediately ensued that she, with laughing face and plundered dress, was borne towards it in the center of a flushed and boisterous group, just in time to greet the father, who came home attended by a man laden with Christmas toys and presents. Then the shouting and the struggling, and the onslaught that was made on the defenseless porter! The scaling him, with chairs for ladders, to dive into his pockets, despoil him of brown-paper parcels, hold on tight by his cravat, hug him round the neck, pummel his back, and kick his legs in irrepressible affection! The shouts of wonder and delight with which the development of every package was received! The terrible announcement that the baby had been taken in the act of putting a doll's frying-pan into his mouth, and was more than suspected of having swallowed a fictitious turkey, glued on a wooden platter! The immense relief of finding this a false alarm! The joy, and gratitude, and ecstasy! They are all indescribable alike. It is enough that by degrees, the children and their emotions got out of the parlor, and, by one stair at a time, up to the top of the house, where they went to bed, and so subsided.

And now Scrooge looked on more attentively than ever, when the master of the house, having his daughter leaning fondly on him, sat down with her and her mother at his own fireside; and when he thought that such another creature, quite as graceful and as full of promise, might have called him father, and been a springtime in the haggard winter of his life, his sight grew very dim indeed.

"Belle," said the husband, turning to his wife with a smile, "I saw an old friend of yours this afternoon."

"Who was it?"

"Guess!"

"How can I? Tut, don't I know?" she added in the same breath, laughing as he laughed. "Mr. Scrooge."

"Mr. Scrooge it was. I passed his office window; and as it was not shut up, and he had a candle inside, I could scarcely help seeing him.

His partner lies upon the point of death, I hear; and there he sat alone. Quite alone in the world, I do believe."

"Spirit!" said Scrooge in a broken voice, "Remove me from this place."

"I told you these were shadows of the things that have been," said the Ghost. "That they are what they are, do not blame me!"

"Remove me!" Scrooge exclaimed. "I cannot bear it!"

He turned upon the Ghost, and seeing that it looked upon him with a face in which in some strange way there were fragments of all the faces it had shown him, wrestled with it.

"Leave me! Take me back! Haunt me no longer!"

In the struggle—if that can be called a struggle in which the Ghost, with no visible resistance on its own part, was undisturbed by any effort of its adversary—Scrooge observed that its light was burning high and bright; and dimly connecting that with its influence over him, he seized the extinguisher cap, and by a sudden action pressed it down upon its head.

The Spirit dropped beneath it, so that the extinguisher covered its whole form; but, though Scrooge pressed it down with all his force, he could not hide the light, which streamed from under it in an unbroken flood upon the ground.

He was conscious of being exhausted, and overcome by an irresistible drowsiness; and, further, of being in his own bedroom. He gave the cap a parting squeeze, in which his hand relaxed; and had barely time to reel to bed before he sank into a heavy sleep.

For the love of money is the root of all evil: which while some coveted after, they have erred from the faith, and pierced themselves through with many sorrows. (1 Timothy 6:10)

Discussion Question:
How did seeking money affect Scrooge's happiness? Why did it overcome his life?

December 12

AWAKING IN THE MIDDLE of a prodigiously tough snore, and sitting up in bed to get his thoughts together, Scrooge had no occasion to be told that the bell was again upon the stroke of One. He felt that he was restored to consciousness in the right nick of time, for the especial purpose of holding a conference with the second messenger dispatched to him through Jacob Marley's intervention. But, finding that he turned uncomfortably cold when he began to wonder which of his curtains this new specter would draw back, he put them every one aside with his own hands, and, lying down again, established a sharp look-out all round the bed. For he wished to challenge the Spirit on the moment of its appearance, and did not wish to be taken by surprise and made nervous.

CHARLES DICKENS

Gentlemen of the free-and-easy sort, who plume themselves on being acquainted with a move or two, and being usually equal to the time of day, express the wide range of their capacity for adventure by observing that they are good for anything from pitch-and-toss to manslaughter; between which opposite extremes, no doubt, there lies a tolerably wide and comprehensive range of subjects. Without venturing for Scrooge quite as hardily as this, I don't mind calling on you to believe that he was ready for a good broad field of strange appearances, and that nothing between a baby and a rhinoceros would have astonished him very much.

Now, being prepared for almost anything, he was not by any means prepared for nothing; and consequently, when the bell struck One, and no shape appeared, he was taken with a violent fit of trembling. Five minutes, ten minutes, a quarter of an hour went by, yet nothing came. All this time he lay upon his bed, the very core and center of a blaze of ruddy light, which streamed upon it when the clock proclaimed the hour; and which, being only light, was more alarming than a dozen ghosts, as he was powerless to make out what it meant, or would be at; and was sometimes apprehensive that he might be at that very moment an interesting case of spontaneous combustion, without having the consolation of knowing it. At last, however, he began to think—as you or I would have thought at first; for it is always the person not in the predicament who knows what ought to have been done in it, and would unquestionably have done it too—at last, I say, he began to think that the source and secret of this ghostly light might be in the adjoining room, from whence, on further tracing it, it seemed to shine. This idea taking full possession of his mind, he got up softly, and shuffled in his slippers to the door.

The moment Scrooge's hand was on the lock, a strange voice called him by his name, and bade him enter. He obeyed.

It was his own room. There was no doubt about that. But it had undergone a surprising transformation. The walls and ceiling were so hung with living green, that it looked a perfect grove; from every part of which bright gleaming berries glistened. The crisp leaves of holly, mistletoe, and ivy reflected back the light, as if so many little mirrors had been scattered there; and such a mighty blaze went roaring up the chimney as that dull petrifaction of a hearth had never known in Scrooge's time, or Marley's, or for many and many a winter season gone.

Heaped up on the floor, to form a kind of throne, were turkeys, geese, game, poultry, brawn,[1] great joints of meat, sucking-pigs, long wreaths of sausages, mince pies, plum puddings, barrels of oysters, red-hot chestnuts, cherry-cheeked apples, juicy oranges, luscious pears, immense twelfth-cakes, and seething bowls of punch, that made the chamber dim with their delicious steam. In easy state upon this couch there sat a jolly Giant, glorious to see; who bore a glowing torch, in shape not unlike Plenty's horn, and held it up, high up, to shed its light on Scrooge as he came peeping round the door.

"Come in!" exclaimed the Ghost. "Come in! And know me better, man!"

Scrooge entered timidly, and hung his head before this Spirit. He was not the dogged Scrooge he had been; and, though the Spirit's eyes were clear and kind, he did not like to meet them.

"I am the Ghost of Christmas Present," said the Spirit. "Look upon me!"

Scrooge reverently did so. It was clothed in one simple deep green robe, or mantle, bordered with white fur. This garment hung so

---

[1] flesh from a pig's or calf's head that is cooked and pressed in a pot with jelly

loosely on the figure, that its capacious breast was bare, as if disdaining to be warded or concealed by any artifice. Its feet, observable beneath the ample folds of the garment, were also bare; and on its head it wore no other covering than a holly wreath, set here and there with shining icicles. Its dark brown curls were long and free; free as its genial face, its sparkling eye, its open hand, its cheery voice, its unconstrained demeanor, and its joyful air. Girded round its middle was an antique scabbard; but no sword was in it, and the ancient sheath was eaten up with rust.

"You have never seen the like of me before!" exclaimed the Spirit.

"Never," Scrooge made answer to it.

"Have never walked forth with the younger members of my family; meaning (for I am very young) my elder brothers born in these later years?" pursued the Phantom.

"I don't think I have," said Scrooge. "I am afraid I have not. Have you had many brothers, Spirit?"

"More than eighteen hundred," said the Ghost.

"A tremendous family to provide for," muttered Scrooge.

The Ghost of Christmas Present rose.

"Spirit," said Scrooge submissively, "conduct me where you will. I went forth last night on compulsion, and I learned a lesson which is working now. Tonight, if you have aught to teach me, let me profit by it."

"Touch my robe!"

Scrooge did as he was told, and held it fast.

Glory to God in the highest, and on earth peace, good will toward men. (Luke 2:14)

Discussion Question:
How do you picture the Christmas spirit?

December 13

HOLLY, MISTLETOE, RED BERRIES, ivy, turkeys, geese, game, poultry, brawn, meat, pigs, sausages, oysters, pies, puddings, fruit, and punch, all vanished instantly. So did the room, the fire, the ruddy glow, the hour of night, and they stood in the city streets on Christmas morning, where (for the weather was severe) the people made a rough, but brisk and not unpleasant kind of music, in scraping the snow from the pavement in front of their dwellings, and from the tops of their houses, whence it was mad delight to the boys to see it come plumping down into the road below, and splitting into artificial little snow-storms.

The house fronts looked black enough, and the windows blacker, contrasting with the smooth white sheet of snow upon the roofs, and with the dirtier snow upon the ground;

which last deposit had been plowed up in deep furrows by the heavy wheels of carts and wagons; furrows that crossed and recrossed each other hundreds of times where the great streets branched off; and made intricate channels, hard to trace, in the thick yellow mud and icy water. The sky was gloomy, and the shortest streets were choked up with a dingy mist, half thawed, half frozen, whose heavier particles descended in a shower of sooty atoms, as if all the chimneys in Great Britain had, by one consent, caught fire, and were blazing away to their dear hearts' content. There was nothing very cheerful in the climate or the town, and yet was there an air of cheerfulness abroad that the clearest summer air and brightest summer sun might have endeavored to diffuse in vain.

For, the people who were shoveling away on the housetops were jovial and full of glee; calling out to one another from the parapets, and now and then exchanging a facetious snowball—better-natured missile far than many a wordy jest—laughing heartily if it went right, and not less heartily if it went wrong. The poulterers' shops were still half open, and the fruiterers' were radiant in their glory. There were great, round, pot-bellied baskets of chestnuts, shaped like the waistcoats of jolly old gentlemen, lolling at the doors, and tumbling out into the street in their apoplectic opulence. There were ruddy, brown-faced, broad-girthed Spanish onions, shining in the fatness of their growth like Spanish Friars, and winking from their shelves in wanton slyness at the girls as they went by, and glanced demurely at the hung-up mistletoe. There were pears and apples clustered high in blooming pyramids; there were bunches of grapes, made, in the shopkeepers' benevolence, to dangle from conspicuous hooks that people's mouths might water gratis as they passed; there were piles of filberts, mossy and brown, recalling, in their fragrance, ancient walks among the woods, and pleasant shufflings ankle deep through withered leaves; there were Norfolk Biffins,[1] squab and swarthy, setting off the yellow of the oranges and lemons, and, in the great compactness of their juicy persons, urgently entreating and beseeching to be carried home in paper bags, and eaten after dinner. The very gold and silver fish, set forth among these choice fruits in a bowl, though members of a dull and stagnant-blooded race, appeared to know that there was something going on; and, to a fish, went gasping round and round their little world in slow and passionless excitement.

---

[1] a variety of apple

CHARLES DICKENS

The Grocers'! Oh, the Grocers'! Nearly closed, with perhaps two shutters down, or one; but through those gaps such glimpses! It was not alone that the scales descending on the counter made a merry sound, or that the twine and roller parted company so briskly, or that the canisters were rattled up and down like juggling tricks, or even that the blended scents of tea and coffee were so grateful to the nose, or even that the raisins were so plentiful and rare, the almonds so extremely white, the sticks of cinnamon so long and straight, the other spices so delicious, the candied fruits so caked and spotted with molten sugar as to make the coldest lookers-on feel faint, and subsequently bilious. Nor was it that the figs were moist and pulpy, or that the French plums blushed in modest tartness from their highly-decorated boxes, or that everything was good to eat and in its Christmas dress; but the customers were all so hurried and so eager in the hopeful promise of the day, that they tumbled up against each other at the door, crashing their wicker baskets wildly, and left their purchases upon the counter, and came running back to fetch them, and committed hundreds of the like mistakes, in the best humor possible; while the Grocer and his people were so frank and fresh, that the polished hearts with which they fastened their aprons behind might have been their own, worn outside for general inspection, and for Christmas daws to peck at if they chose.

But soon the steeples called good people all to church and chapel, and away they came, flocking through the streets in their best clothes, and with their gayest faces. And at the same time there emerged, from scores of by-streets, lanes, and nameless turnings, innumerable people, carrying their dinners to the bakers' shops. The sight of these poor revelers appeared to interest the Spirit very much, for he stood with Scrooge beside him in a baker's doorway, and, taking off the covers as their bearers passed, sprinkled incense on their dinners from his torch. And it was a very uncommon kind of torch, for once or twice, when there were angry words between some dinner-carriers who had jostled each other, he shed a few drops of water on them from it, and their good humor was restored directly. For they said, it was a shame to quarrel upon Christmas Day. And so it was! God love it, so it was!

In time the bells ceased, and the bakers were shut up; and yet there was a genial shadowing forth of all these dinners, and the progress of their cooking, in the thawed blotch of wet above each baker's oven; where the pavement smoked as if its stones were cooking too.

"Is there a peculiar flavor in what you sprinkle from your torch?" asked Scrooge.

"There is. My own."

"Would it apply to any kind of dinner on this day?" asked Scrooge.

"To any kindly given. To a poor one most."

"Why to a poor one most?" asked Scrooge.

"Because it needs it most."

"Spirit!" said Scrooge after a moment's thought. "I wonder you, of all the beings in the many worlds about us, should desire to cramp these people's opportunities of innocent enjoyment."

"I!" cried the Spirit.

"You would deprive them of their means of dining every seventh day, often the only day on which they can be said to dine at all," said Scrooge; "wouldn't you?"[1]

"I!" cried the Spirit.

---

[1] The poor did not have their own ovens, and as outlined in the vision above, the bakers (who were prohibited from baking on the Sabbath) would open their doors to the people to come heat their dinners in the commercial ovens.

"You seek to close these places on the Seventh Day," said Scrooge. "And it comes to the same thing."

"I seek!" exclaimed the Spirit.

"Forgive me if I am wrong. It has been done in your name, or at least in that of your family," said Scrooge.

"There are some upon this earth of yours," returned the Spirit, "who lay claim to know us, and who do their deeds of passion, pride, ill-will, hatred, envy, bigotry, and selfishness in our name, who are as strange to us, and all our kith and kin, as if they had never lived. Remember that, and charge their doings on themselves, not us."

Scrooge promised that he would; and they went on, invisible, as they had been before, into the suburbs of the town. It was a remarkable quality of the Ghost (which Scrooge had observed at the baker's), that, notwithstanding his gigantic size, he could accommodate himself to any place with ease; and that he stood beneath a low roof quite as gracefully and like a supernatural creature as it was possible he could have done in any lofty hall.

But ye have despised the poor. Do not rich men oppress you, and draw you before the judgment seats? (James 2:6)

CHARLES DICKENS

Discussion Question:
What other things are done in the name of God or religion that are oppressive to the people.

December 14

AND PERHAPS IT WAS the pleasure the good Spirit had in showing off this power of his, or else it was his own kind, generous, hearty nature, and his sympathy with all poor men, that led him straight to Scrooge's clerk's; for there he went, and took Scrooge with him, holding to his robe; and, on the threshold of the door, the Spirit smiled, and stopped to bless Bob Cratchit's dwelling with the sprinklings of his torch. Think of that! Bob had but fifteen "Bob" a week himself; he pocketed on Saturdays but fifteen copies of his Christian name; and yet the Ghost of Christmas Present blessed his four-roomed house!

Then up rose Mrs. Cratchit, Cratchit's wife, dressed out but poorly in a twice-turned gown, but brave in ribbons, which are cheap, and make a goodly show for sixpence; and she laid the cloth, assisted by Belinda Cratchit, second of her daughters, also brave in ribbons; while Master Peter Cratchit plunged a fork into the saucepan of potatoes, and, getting the corners of his monstrous shirt-collar (Bob's private property, conferred upon his son and heir in honor of the day) into his mouth, rejoiced to find himself so gallantly attired, and yearned to show his linen in the fashionable Parks. And now two smaller Cratchits, boy and girl, came tearing in, screaming that outside the baker's they had smelt the goose, and known it for their own; and, basking in luxurious thoughts of sage and onion, these young Cratchits danced about the table, and exalted Master Peter Cratchit to the skies, while he (not proud, although his collars nearly choked him) blew the fire, until the slow potatoes, bubbling up, knocked loudly at the saucepan-lid to be let out and peeled.

"What has ever got your precious father, then?" said Mrs. Cratchit. "And your brother, Tiny Tim? And Martha warn't as late last Christmas Day by half an hour!"

"Here's Martha, mother!" said a girl, appearing as she spoke.

"Here's Martha, mother!" cried the two young Cratchits. "Hurrah! There's such a goose, Martha!"

"Why, bless your heart alive, my dear, how late you are!" said Mrs. Cratchit, kissing her a dozen times, and taking off her shawl and bonnet for her with officious zeal.

"We'd a deal of work to finish up last night," replied the girl, "and had to clear away this morning, mother!"

"Well! Never mind so long as you are come," said Mrs. Cratchit. "Sit ye down before the fire, my dear, and have a warm, Lord bless ye!"

"No, no! There's father coming," cried the two young Cratchits, who were everywhere at once. "Hide, Martha, hide!"

So Martha hid herself, and in came little Bob, the father, with at least three feet of comforter, exclusive of the fringe, hanging down before him; and his threadbare clothes darned up and brushed to look seasonable; and Tiny Tim upon his shoulder. Alas for Tiny Tim, he bore a little crutch, and had his limbs supported by an iron frame!

"Why, where's our Martha?" cried Bob Cratchit, looking round.

"Not coming," said Mrs. Cratchit.

"Not coming!" said Bob with a sudden declension in his high spirits; for he had been Tim's blood horse all the way from church, and had come home rampant. "Not coming upon Christmas Day!"

Martha didn't like to see him disappointed, if it were only in joke; so she came out prematurely from behind the closet door, and ran into his arms, while the two young Cratchits hustled Tiny Tim, and bore him off into the wash house, that he might hear the pudding singing in the copper.

"And how did little Tim behave?" asked Mrs. Cratchit when she had rallied Bob on his credulity, and Bob had hugged his daughter to his heart's content.

"As good as gold," said Bob, "and better. Somehow, he gets thoughtful, sitting by himself so much, and thinks the strangest things you ever heard. He told me, coming home, that he hoped the people saw him in the church, because he was a cripple, and it might be pleasant to them to remember upon Christmas Day who made lame beggars walk and blind men see."

Bob's voice was tremulous when he told them this, and trembled more when he said that Tiny Tim was growing strong and hearty.

His active little crutch was heard upon the floor, and back came Tiny Tim before another word was spoken, escorted by his brother and sister to his stool beside the fire; and while Bob, turning up his cuffs—as if, poor fellow, they were capable of being made more shabby—compounded some hot mixture in a jug with gin and lemons, and stirred it round and round, and put it on the hob to simmer, Master Peter and the two ubiquitous young Cratchits went to fetch the goose, with which they soon returned in high procession.

Such a bustle ensued that you might have thought a goose the rarest of all birds; a feathered phenomenon, to which a black swan was a matter of course—and, in truth, it was something very like it in that house. Mrs. Cratchit made the gravy (ready beforehand in a little saucepan) hissing hot; Master Peter mashed the potatoes with incredible vigor; Miss Belinda sweetened up the applesauce; Martha dusted the hot plates; Bob took Tiny Tim beside him in a tiny corner at the table; the two young Cratchits set chairs for everybody, not forgetting themselves, and, mounting guard upon their posts, crammed spoons into their mouths, lest they should shriek for goose before their turn came to be helped. At last the dishes were set on, and grace was said. It was succeeded by a breathless pause, as Mrs. Cratchit, looking slowly all along the carving knife, prepared to plunge it in the breast; but when she did, and when the long-expected gush of stuffing issued forth, one murmur of delight arose all round the board, and even Tiny Tim, excited by the two young Cratchits, beat on the table with the handle of his knife, and feebly cried Hurrah!

There never was such a goose. Bob said he didn't believe there ever was such a goose cooked. Its tenderness and flavor, size and cheapness, were the themes of universal admiration. Eked out by applesauce and mashed potatoes, it was a sufficient dinner for the whole family; indeed, as Mrs. Cratchit said with great delight (surveying one small atom of a bone upon the dish), they hadn't ate it all at last! Yet everyone had had enough, and the youngest Cratchits, in particular, were steeped in sage and onion to the eyebrows! But now, the plates being changed by Miss Belinda, Mrs. Cratchit left the room alone—too nervous to bear witnesses—to take the pudding up, and bring it in.

Suppose it should not be done enough! Suppose it should break in turning out! Suppose somebody should have got over the wall of the back-yard and stolen it, while they were merry with the goose—a supposition at which the two young Cratchits became livid! All sorts of horrors were supposed.

Hallo! A great deal of steam! The pudding was out of the copper. A smell like a washing-day! That was the cloth. A smell like an eating-house and a pastry cook's next door to each other, with a laundress's next door to that! That was the pudding! In half a minute Mrs. Cratchit entered—flushed, but smiling proudly—with the pudding, like a speckled cannon-ball, so hard and firm, blazing in half of half-a-quartern of ignited brandy, and bedight with Christmas holly stuck into the top.

Oh, a wonderful pudding! Bob Cratchit said, and calmly too, that he regarded it as the greatest success achieved by Mrs. Cratchit since their marriage. Mrs. Cratchit said that, now the weight was off her mind, she would confess she had her doubts about the quantity of flour. Everybody had something to say about it, but nobody said or thought it was at all a small pudding for a large family. It would have been flat heresy to do so. Any Cratchit would have blushed to hint at such a thing.

At last the dinner was all done, the cloth was cleared, the hearth swept, and the fire made up. The compound in the jug being tasted, and considered perfect, apples and oranges were put upon the table, and a shovel full of chestnuts on the fire. Then all the Cratchit family drew round the hearth in what Bob Cratchit called a circle, meaning half a one; and at Bob Cratchit's elbow stood the family display of glass. Two tumblers and a custard cup without a handle.

These held the hot stuff from the jug, however, as well as golden goblets would have done; and Bob served it out with beaming looks, while the chestnuts on the fire sputtered and cracked noisily. Then Bob proposed:

"A merry Christmas to us all, my dears. God bless us!"

Which all the family re-echoed.

"God bless us every one!" said Tiny Tim, the last of all.

He sat very close to his father's side, upon his little stool. Bob held his withered little hand in his, as if he loved the child, and wished to keep him by his side, and dreaded that he might be taken from him.

Then was brought unto him one possessed with a devil, blind, and dumb: and he healed him, insomuch that the blind and dumb both spake and saw. (Matthew 12:22)

Discussion Question:
How does the Cratchit's dinner compare to you traditional Christmas dinner?

December 15

PIRIT," SAID SCROOGE WITH an interest he had never felt before, "tell me if Tiny Tim will live."

"I see a vacant seat," replied the Ghost, "in the poor chimney-corner, and a crutch without an owner, carefully preserved. If these shadows remain unaltered by the Future, the child will die."

"No, no," said Scrooge. "Oh, no, kind Spirit! Say he will be spared."

"If these shadows remain unaltered by the Future, none other of my race," returned the Ghost, "will find him here. What then? If he be like to die, he had better do it, and decrease the surplus population."

Scrooge hung his head to hear his own words quoted by the Spirit, and was overcome with penitence and grief.

"Man," said the Ghost, "if man you be in heart, not adamant, forbear that wicked cant until you have discovered What the surplus is, and Where it is. Will you decide what men shall live, what men shall die? It may be that, in the sight of Heaven, you are more worthless and less fit to live than millions like this poor man's child. Oh God! To hear the Insect on the leaf pronouncing on the too much life among his hungry brothers in the dust!"

Scrooge bent before the Ghost's rebuke, and, trembling, cast his eyes upon the ground. But he raised them speedily on hearing his own name.

"Mr. Scrooge!" said Bob. "I'll give you Mr. Scrooge, the Founder of the Feast!"

"The Founder of the Feast, indeed!" cried Mrs. Cratchit, reddening. "I wish I had him here. I'd give him a piece of my mind to feast upon, and I hope he'd have a good appetite for it."

"My dear," said Bob, "the children! Christmas Day."

"It should be Christmas Day, I am sure," said she, "on which one drinks the health of such an odious, stingy, hard, unfeeling man as Mr. Scrooge. You know he is, Robert! Nobody knows it better than you do, poor fellow!"

"My dear!" was Bob's mild answer. "Christmas Day."

"I'll drink his health for your sake and the Day's," said Mrs. Cratchit, "not for his. Long life to him! A merry Christmas and a happy New Year! He'll be very merry and very happy, I have no doubt!"

The children drank the toast after her. It was the first of their proceedings which had no heartiness in it. Tiny Tim drank it last of all, but he didn't care twopence for it. Scrooge was the Ogre of the family. The mention of his name cast a dark shadow on the party, which was not dispelled for full five minutes.

After it had passed away they were ten times merrier than before, from the mere relief of Scrooge the Baleful being done with. Bob Cratchit told them how he had a situation in his eye for Master Peter, which would bring in, if obtained, full five-and-sixpence weekly. The two young Cratchits laughed tremendously at the idea of Peter's being a man of business; and Peter himself looked thoughtfully at the fire from between his collars, as if he were deliberating what particular investments he should favor when he came into the receipt of that bewildering income. Martha, who was a poor apprentice at a milliner's, then told them what kind of work she had to do, and how many hours she worked at a stretch, and how she meant to lie abed tomorrow morning for a good long rest; tomorrow being a holiday she passed at home. Also how she had seen a countess and a lord some days before, and how the lord "was much about as tall as Peter"; at which Peter pulled up his collars so high, that you couldn't have seen his head if you had been there. All this time the chestnuts and the jug went round and round; and by-and-by they had a song, about a lost child traveling in the snow, from Tiny Tim, who had a plaintive little voice, and sang it very well indeed.

There was nothing of high mark in this. They were not a handsome family; they were not well dressed; their shoes were far from being waterproof; their clothes were scanty; and Peter might have known, and very likely did, the inside of a pawn-broker's. But they were happy, grateful, pleased with one another, and contented with the time; and when they faded, and looked happier yet in the bright sprinklings of the Spirit's torch at parting, Scrooge had his eye upon them, and especially on Tiny Tim, until the last.

By this time it was getting dark, and snowing pretty heavily; and as Scrooge and the Spirit went along the streets, the brightness of the roaring fires in kitchens, parlors, and all sorts of rooms was wonderful. Here, the flickering of the blaze showed preparations for a cozy dinner, with hot plates baking through and through before the fire, and deep red curtains, ready to be drawn to shut out cold and darkness. There, all the children of the house were running out into the snow to meet their married sisters, brothers, cousins, uncles, aunts, and be the first to greet them. Here, again, were shadows on the window blinds of guests assembling; and there a group of handsome girls, all hooded and fur-booted, and all chattering at once, tripped lightly off to some near neighbor's house; where, woe upon the single man who saw them enter—artful witches, well they knew it—in a glow!

But, if you had judged from the numbers of people on their way to friendly gatherings, you might have thought that no one was at home to give them welcome when they got there, instead of every house expecting company, and piling up its fires half-chimney high. Blessings on it, how the Ghost exulted! How it bared its breadth of breast, and opened its capacious palm, and floated on, outpouring, with a generous hand, its bright and harmless mirth on everything within its reach! The very lamplighter, who ran on before, dotting the dusky street with specks of light, and who was dressed to spend the evening somewhere, laughed out loudly as the Spirit passed, though little kenned the lamp-lighter that he had any company but Christmas.

Ye shall be sorrowful, but your sorrow shall be turned into joy. (John 16:20)

Discussion Question:
Why should or shouldn't the Cratchits toast Scrooge?

December 16

AND NOW, WITHOUT A word of warning from the Ghost, they stood upon a bleak and desert moor, where monstrous masses of rude stone were cast about, as though it were the burial place or giants; and water spread itself wheresoever it listed; or would have done so, but for the frost that held it prisoner; and nothing grew but moss and furze, and coarse, rank grass. Down in the west the setting sun had left a streak of fiery red, which glared upon the desolation for an instant, like a sullen eye, and, frowning lower, lower, lower yet, was lost in the thick gloom of darkest night.

"What place is this?" asked Scrooge.

"A place where Miners live, who labor in the bowels of the earth," returned the Spirit. "But they know me. See!"

A light shone from the window of a hut, and swiftly they advanced towards it. Passing through the wall of mud and stone, they found a cheerful company assembled round a glowing fire. An old, old man and woman, with their children and their children's children, and another generation beyond that, all decked out gaily in their holiday attire. The old man, in a voice that seldom rose above the howling of the wind upon the barren waste, was singing them a Christmas song; it had been a very old song when he was a boy; and from time to time they all joined in the chorus. So surely as they raised their voices, the old man got quite blithe and loud; and, so surely as they stopped, his vigor sank again.

The Spirit did not tarry here, but bade Scrooge hold his robe, and, passing on above the moor, sped whither? Not to sea? To sea. To Scrooge's horror, looking back, he saw the last of the land, a frightful range of rocks, behind them; and his ears were deafened by the thundering of water, as it rolled and roared, and raged among the dreadful caverns it had worn, and fiercely tried to undermine the earth.

Built upon a dismal reef of sunken rocks, some league or so from shore, on which the waters chafed and dashed, the wild year through, there stood a solitary lighthouse. Great heaps of seaweed clung to its base, and stormbirds—born of the wind, one might suppose, as seaweed of the water—rose and fell about it, like the waves they skimmed.

But, even here, two men who watched the light had made a fire that through the loophole in the thick stone wall shed out a ray of brightness on the awful sea. Joining their horny hands over the rough table at which they sat, they wished each other Merry Christmas in their can of grog; and one of them, the elder too, with his face all damaged and scarred with hard weather, as the figure-head of an old ship might be, struck up a sturdy song that was like a gale in itself.

Again the Ghost sped on, above the black and heaving sea—on, on—until, being far away, as he told Scrooge, from any shore, they lighted on a ship. They stood beside the helmsman at the wheel, the look-out in the bow, the officers who had the watch; dark, ghostly figures in their several stations; but every man among them hummed a Christmas tune, or had a Christmas thought, or spoke below his breath to his companion of some bygone Christmas Day, with homeward hopes belonging to it. And every man on board, waking or sleeping, good or bad, had had a kinder word for one another on that day than on any day in the year;

and had shared to some extent in its festivities; and had remembered those he cared for at a distance, and had known that they delighted to remember him.

It was a great surprise to Scrooge, while listening to the moaning of the wind, and thinking what a solemn thing it was to move on through the lonely darkness over an unknown abyss, whose depths were secrets as profound as death: it was a great surprise to Scrooge, while thus engaged, to hear a hearty laugh. It was a much greater surprise to Scrooge to recognize it as his own nephew's, and to find himself in a bright, dry, gleaming room, with the Spirit standing smiling by his side, and looking at that same nephew with approving affability!

"Ha, ha!" laughed Scrooge's nephew. "Ha, ha, ha!"

If you should happen, by any unlikely chance, to know a man more blessed in a laugh than Scrooge's nephew, all I can say is, I should like to know him too. Introduce him to me, and I'll cultivate his acquaintance.

It is a fair, even-handed, noble adjustment of things, that, while there is infection in disease and sorrow, there is nothing in the world so irresistibly contagious as laughter and good humor. When Scrooge's nephew laughed in this way, holding his sides, rolling his head, and twisting his face into the most extravagant contortions, Scrooge's niece, by marriage, laughed as heartily as he. And their assembled friends, being not a bit behindhand, roared out lustily.

"Ha, ha! Ha, ha, ha, ha!"

"He said that Christmas was a humbug, as I live!" cried Scrooge's nephew. "He believed it, too!"

"More shame for him, Fred!" said Scrooge's niece indignantly. Bless those women! They never do anything by halves. They are always in earnest.

She was very pretty; exceedingly pretty. With a dimpled, surprised-looking, capital face; a ripe little mouth, that seemed made to be kissed—as no doubt it was; all kinds of good little dots about her chin, that melted into one another when she laughed; and the sunniest pair of eyes you ever saw in any little creature's head. Altogether she was what you would have called provoking, you know; but satisfactory, too. Oh, perfectly satisfactory!

"He's a comical old fellow," said Scrooge's nephew, "that's the truth; and not so pleasant as he might be. However, his offenses carry their own punishment, and I have nothing to say against him."

CHARLES DICKENS

"I'm sure he is very rich, Fred," hinted Scrooge's niece. "At least, you always tell me so."

"What of that, my dear?" said Scrooge's nephew. "His wealth is of no use to him. He don't do any good with it. He don't make himself comfortable with it. He hasn't the satisfaction of thinking—ha, ha, ha!—that he is ever going to benefit Us with it."

God anointed Jesus of Nazareth with the Holy Ghost and with power: who went about doing good, and healing all that were oppressed of the devil; for God was with him. (Acts 10:38)

Discussion Question:

These scenes are often missed from retellings and movies of The Christmas Carol. What do the miners and sailors have to be happy about at Christmas?

December 17

"I HAVE NO PATIENCE with him," observed Scrooge's niece.

Scrooge's niece's sisters, and all the other ladies, expressed the same opinion.

"Oh, I have!" said Scrooge's nephew. "I am sorry for him; I couldn't be angry with him if I tried. Who suffers by his ill whims? Himself always. Here he takes it into his head to dislike us, and he won't come and dine with us. What's the consequence? He don't lose much of a dinner."

"Indeed, I think he loses a very good dinner," interrupted Scrooge's niece. Everybody else said the same, and they must be allowed to have been competent judges, because they had just had dinner; and, with the dessert upon the table, were clustered round the fire, by lamplight.

"Well! I am very glad to hear it," said Scrooge's nephew, "because I haven't any great faith in these young housekeepers. What do you say, Topper?"

Topper had clearly got his eye upon one of Scrooge's niece's sisters, for he answered that a bachelor was a wretched outcast, who had no right to express an opinion on the subject. Whereat Scrooge's niece's sister—the plump one with the lace tucker, not the one with the roses—blushed.

"Do go on, Fred," said Scrooge's niece, clapping her hands. "He never finishes what he begins to say! He is such a ridiculous fellow!"

Scrooge's nephew reveled in another laugh, and, as it was impossible to keep the infection off, though the plump sister tried hard to do it with aromatic vinegar, his example was unanimously followed.

"I was only going to say," said Scrooge's nephew, "that the consequence of his taking a dislike to us, and not making merry with us, is, as I think, that he loses some pleasant moments, which could do him no harm. I am sure he loses pleasanter companions than he can find in his own thoughts, either in his moldy old office or his dusty chambers. I mean to give him the same chance every year, whether he likes it or not, for I pity him. He may rail at Christmas till he dies, but he can't help thinking better of it—I defy him—if he finds me going there in good temper, year after year, and saying, 'Uncle Scrooge, how are you?' If it only puts him in the vein to leave his poor clerk fifty pounds, that's something; and I think I shook him yesterday."

It was their turn to laugh, now, at the notion of his shaking Scrooge. But, being thoroughly good-natured, and not much caring what they laughed at, so that they laughed at any rate, he encouraged them in their merriment, and passed the bottle, joyously.

After tea they had some music. For they were a musical family, and knew what they were about when they sung a Glee[1] or Catch,[2] I can assure you: especially Topper, who could growl away in the bass like a good one, and never swell the large veins in his forehead, or get red in the face over it. Scrooge's niece played well upon the harp; and played, among other tunes, a simple little air (a mere nothing: you might learn to whistle it in two minutes), which had been familiar to the child who fetched Scrooge

---

[1] A three or four voice song sung a cappella (without musical accompaniment).
[2] A round, intended to be sung repeatedly, beginning at different times.

from the boarding-school, as he had been reminded by the Ghost of Christmas Past. When this strain of music sounded, all the things that Ghost had shown him came upon his mind; he softened more and more; and thought that if he could have listened to it often, years ago, he might have cultivated the kindnesses of life for his own happiness with his own hands, without resorting to the sexton's spade that buried Jacob Marley.

But they didn't devote the whole evening to music. After awhile they played at forfeits; for it is good to be children sometimes, and never better than at Christmas, when its mighty Founder was a child himself. Stop! There was first a game at blind man's buff. Of course there was. And I no more believe Topper was really blind than I believe he had eyes in his boots. My opinion is, that it was a done thing between him and Scrooge's nephew; and that the Ghost of Christmas Present knew it. The way he went after that plump sister in the lace tucker was an outrage on the credulity of human nature. Knocking down the fire-irons, tumbling over the chairs, bumping up against the piano, smothering himself amongst the curtains, wherever she went, there went he! He always knew where the plump sister was. He wouldn't catch anybody else. If you had fallen up against him (as some of them did) on purpose, he would have made a feint of endeavoring to seize you, which would have been an affront to your understanding, and would instantly have sidled off in the direction of the plump sister. She often cried out that it wasn't fair; and it really was not. But when, at last, he caught her; when, in spite of all her silken rustlings, and her rapid flutterings past him, he got her into a corner whence there was no escape, then his conduct was the most execrable. For his pretending not to know her; his pretending that it was necessary to touch her head-dress, and further to assure himself of her identity by pressing a certain ring upon her finger, and a certain chain about her neck, was vile, monstrous! No doubt she told him her opinion of it when, another blind man being in office, they were so very confidential together behind the curtains.

Scrooge's niece was not one of the blind man's buff party, but was made comfortable with a large chair and a footstool, in a snug corner where the Ghost and Scrooge were close behind her. But she joined in the forfeits, and loved her love to admiration with all the letters of the alphabet. Likewise at the game of How, When, and Where, she was very great, and, to the secret joy of Scrooge's nephew, beat her sisters hollow: though they were sharp girls too, as Topper could have told you. There might have been twenty people there, young and old, but they all played, and so did Scrooge; for, wholly forgetting, in the interest he had in what was going on, that his voice made no sound in their ears, he sometimes came out with his guess quite loud, and very often guessed right, too, for the sharpest needle, best Whitechapel, warranted not to cut in the eye, was not sharper than Scrooge; blunt as he took it in his head to be.

The Ghost was greatly pleased to find him in this mood, and looked upon him with such favor, that he begged like a boy to be allowed to stay until the guests departed. But this the Spirit said could not be done.

I will sing with the spirit, and I will sing with the understanding also. (1 Corinthians 14:15)

Discussion Question:
What holiday songs bring back memories of your youth?

December 18

"HERE IS A NEW game," said Scrooge. "One half-hour, Spirit, only one!"

It was a game called Yes and No, where Scrooge's nephew had to think of something, and the rest must find out what; he only answering to their questions yes or no, as the case was. The brisk fire of questioning to which he was exposed elicited from him that he was thinking of an animal, a live animal, rather a disagreeable animal, a savage animal, an animal that growled and grunted sometimes, and talked sometimes, and lived in London, and walked about the streets, and wasn't made a show of, and wasn't led by anybody, and didn't live in a menagerie, and was never killed in a market, and was not a horse, or an ass, or a cow, or a bull, or a tiger, or a dog, or a pig, or a cat, or a bear. At every fresh question that was put to him, this nephew burst into a fresh roar of laughter; and was so inexpressibly tickled, that he was obliged to get up off the sofa, and stamp. At last the plump sister, falling into a similar state, cried out:

"I have found it out! I know what it is, Fred! I know what it is!"

"What is it?" cried Fred.

"It's your uncle Scro-o-o-o-oge!"

Which it certainly was. Admiration was the universal sentiment, though some objected that the reply to "Is it a bear?" ought to have been "Yes": inasmuch as an answer in the negative was sufficient to have diverted their thoughts from Mr. Scrooge, supposing they had ever had any tendency that way.

"He has given us plenty of merriment, I am sure," said Fred, "and it would be ungrateful not to drink his health. Here is a glass of mulled wine ready to our hand at the moment; and I say, 'Uncle Scrooge!'"

"Well! Uncle Scrooge!" they cried.

"A merry Christmas and a happy New Year to the old man, whatever he is!" said Scrooge's nephew. "He wouldn't take it from me, but may he have it nevertheless. Uncle Scrooge!"

Uncle Scrooge had imperceptibly become so gay and light of heart, that he would have pledged the unconscious company in return, and thanked them in an inaudible speech, if the

Ghost had given him time. But the whole scene passed off in the breath of the last word spoken by his nephew; and he and the Spirit were again upon their travels.

Much they saw, and far they went, and many homes they visited, but always with a happy end. The Spirit stood beside sick beds, and they were cheerful; on foreign lands, and they were close at home; by struggling men, and they were patient in their greater hope; by poverty, and it was rich. In almshouse, hospital, and jail, in misery's every refuge, where vain man in his little brief authority had not made fast the door, and barred the Spirit out, he left his blessing, and taught Scrooge his precepts.

It was a long night, if it were only a night; but Scrooge had his doubts of this, because the Christmas holidays appeared to be condensed into the space of time they passed together. It was strange, too, that, while Scrooge remained unaltered in his outward form, the Ghost grew older, clearly older. Scrooge had observed this change, but never spoke of it, until they left a children's Twelfth-Night party, when, looking at the Spirit as they stood together in an open place, he noticed that its hair was gray.

"Are spirits' lives so short?" asked Scrooge.

"My life upon this globe is very brief," replied the Ghost. "It ends tonight."

"Tonight!" cried Scrooge.

"Tonight at midnight. Hark! The time is drawing near."

The chimes were ringing the three-quarters past eleven at that moment.

"Forgive me if I am not justified in what I ask," said Scrooge, looking intently at the Spirit's robe, "but I see something strange, and not belonging to yourself, protruding from your skirts. Is it a foot or a claw?"

"It might be a claw, for the flesh there is upon it," was the Spirit's sorrowful reply. "Look here."

From the foldings of its robe it brought two children; wretched, abject, frightful, hideous, miserable. They knelt down at its feet, and clung upon the outside of its garment.

"Oh, Man! Look here! Look, look, down here!" exclaimed the Ghost.

They were a boy and girl. Yellow, meager, ragged, scowling, wolfish; but prostrate, too, in their humility. Where graceful youth should have filled their features out, and touched them with its freshest tints, a stale and shriveled hand, like that of age, had pinched, and twisted them, and pulled them into shreds. Where angels might have sat enthroned, devils lurked, and glared out menacing. No change, no degradation, no perversion of humanity, in any grade, through all the mysteries of wonderful creation, has monsters half so horrible and dread.

Scrooge started back, appalled. Having them shown to him in this way, he tried to say they were fine children, but the words choked themselves, rather than be parties to a lie of such enormous magnitude.

"Spirit! Are they yours?" Scrooge could say no more.

"They are Man's," said the Spirit, looking down upon them. "And they cling to me, appealing from their fathers. This boy is Ignorance. This girl is Want. Beware of them both, and all of their degree, but most of all beware this boy, for on his brow I see that written which is Doom, unless the writing be erased. Deny it!" cried the Spirit, stretching out its hand towards the city. "Slander those who tell it ye! Admit it for your factious purposes, and make it worse! And bide the end!"

"Have they no refuge or resource?" cried Scrooge.

"Are there no prisons?" said the Spirit, turning on him for the last time with his own words. "Are there no workhouses?"

The bell struck twelve.

Scrooge looked about him for the Ghost, and saw it not. As the last stroke ceased to vibrate, he remembered the prediction of old Jacob Marley, and, lifting up his eyes, beheld a solemn Phantom, draped and hooded, coming like a mist along the ground towards him.

And the child grew, and waxed strong in spirit, filled with wisdom: and the grace of God was upon him. (Luke 2:40)

Discussion Question:
How can we combat ignorance and want?

December 19

THE PHANTOM SLOWLY, GRAVELY, silently approached. When it came near him, Scrooge bent down upon his knee; for in the very air through which this Spirit moved it seemed to scatter gloom and mystery.

It was shrouded in a deep black garment, which concealed its head, its face, its form, and left nothing of it visible, save one outstretched hand. But for this, it would have been difficult to detach its figure from the night, and separate it from the darkness by which it was surrounded.

He felt that it was tall and stately when it came beside him, and that its mysterious presence filled him with a solemn dread. He knew no more, for the Spirit neither spoke nor moved.

"I am in the presence of the Ghost of Christmas Yet to Come?" said Scrooge.

The Spirit answered not, but pointed onward with its hand.

"You are about to show me shadows of the things that have not happened, but will happen in the time before us," Scrooge pursued. "Is that so, Spirit?"

The upper portion of the garment was contracted for an instant in its folds, as if the Spirit had inclined its head. That was the only answer he received.

Although well-used to ghostly company by this time, Scrooge feared the silent shape so much that his legs trembled beneath him, and he found that he could hardly stand when he prepared to follow it. The Spirit paused a moment, as observing his condition, and giving him time to recover.

But Scrooge was all the worse for this. It thrilled him with a vague uncertain horror to know that, behind the dusky shroud, there were ghostly eyes intently fixed upon him, while he, though he stretched his own to the utmost, could see nothing but a spectral hand and one great heap of black.

"Ghost of the Future!" he exclaimed, "I fear you more than any specter I have seen. But, as I know your purpose is to do me good, and as I hope to live to be another man from what I was, I am prepared to bear you company, and do it with a thankful heart. Will you not speak to me?"

It gave him no reply. The hand was pointed straight before them.

"Lead on!" said Scrooge. "Lead on! The night is waning fast, and it is precious time to me, I know. Lead on, Spirit!"

The phantom moved away as it had come towards him. Scrooge followed in the shadow of its dress, which bore him up, he thought, and carried him along.

They scarcely seemed to enter the City; for the City rather seemed to spring up about them, and encompass them of its own act. But there they were in the heart of it; on 'Change, amongst the merchants; who hurried up and down, and chinked the money in their pockets, and conversed in groups, and looked at their watches, and trifled thoughtfully with their great gold seals; and so forth, as Scrooge had seen them often.

The Spirit stopped beside one little knot of business men. Observing that the hand was pointed to them, Scrooge advanced to listen to their talk.

"No," said a great fat man with a monstrous chin, "I don't know much about it either way. I only know he's dead."

"When did he die?" inquired another.

"Last night, I believe."

"Why, what was the matter with him?" asked a third, taking a vast quantity of snuff out of a very large snuff-box. "I thought he'd never die."

"God knows," said the first with a yawn.

"What has he done with his money?" asked a red-faced gentleman with a pendulous excrescence on the end of his nose, that shook like the gills of a turkey cock.

"I haven't heard," said the man with the large chin, yawning again. "Left it to his company, perhaps. He hasn't left it to me. That's all I know."

This pleasantry was received with a general laugh.

"It's likely to be a very cheap funeral," said the same speaker; "for, upon my life, I don't know of anybody to go to it. Suppose we make up a party, and volunteer?"

"I don't mind going if a lunch is provided," observed the gentleman with the excrescence on his nose. "But I must be fed if I make one."

Another laugh.

"Well, I am the most disinterested among you, after all," said the first speaker, "for I never wear black gloves, and I never eat lunch. But I'll offer to go if anybody else will. When I come to think of it, I'm not at all sure that I

A CHRISTMAS CAROL

wasn't his most particular friend; for we used to stop and speak whenever we met. Bye, bye!"

Speakers and listeners strolled away, and mixed with other groups. Scrooge knew the men, and looked towards the Spirit for an explanation.

The Phantom glided on into a street. Its finger pointed to two persons meeting. Scrooge listened again, thinking that the explanation might lie here.

He knew these men, also, perfectly. They were men of business: very wealthy, and of great importance. He had made a point always of standing well in their esteem: in a business point of view, that is; strictly in a business point of view.

"How are you?" said one.

"How are you?" returned the other.

"Well!" said the first. "Old Scratch[1] has got his own at last, hey?"

"So I am told," returned the second. "Cold, isn't it?"

"Seasonable for Christmastime. You are not a skater, I suppose?"

"No. No. Something else to think of. Good morning!"

---

[1] The devil

Not another word. That was their meeting, their conversation, and their parting.

Scrooge was at first inclined to be surprised that the Spirit should attach importance to conversations apparently so trivial; but, feeling assured that they must have some hidden purpose, he set himself to consider what it was likely to be. They could scarcely be supposed to have any bearing on the death of Jacob, his old partner, for that was Past, and this Ghost's province was the Future. Nor could he think of any one immediately connected with himself, to whom he could apply them. But nothing doubting that, to whomsoever they applied, they had some latent moral for his own improvement, he resolved to treasure up every word he heard, and everything he saw; and especially to observe the shadow of himself when it appeared. For he had an expectation that the conduct of his future self would give him the clue he missed, and would render the solution of these riddles easy.

He looked about in that very place for his own image, but another man stood in his accustomed corner, and, though the clock pointed to his usual time of day for being there, he saw no likeness of himself among the multitudes that poured in through the Porch. It gave him little surprise, however; for he had been revolving in his mind a change of life, and thought and hoped he saw his new-born resolutions carried out in this.

Quiet and dark, beside him stood the Phantom, with its outstretched hand. When he roused himself from his thoughtful quest, he fancied, from the turn of the hand, and its situation in reference to himself, that the Unseen Eyes were looking at him keenly. It made him shudder, and feel very cold.

For now we see through a glass, darkly; but then face to face: now I know in part; but then shall I know even as also I am known. (1 Corinthians 13:12)

Discussion Question:
What would you want other people to say about you at your funeral? What are you doing to make yourself into that person?

December 20

HEY LEFT THE BUSY scene, and went into an obscure part of the town, where Scrooge had never penetrated before, although he recognized its situation and its bad repute. The ways were foul and narrow; the shops and houses wretched; the people half-naked, drunken, slipshod, ugly. Alleys and archways, like so many cesspools, disgorged their offenses of smell, and dirt, and life upon the straggling streets; and the whole quarter reeked with crime, with filth and misery.

Far in this den of infamous resort, there was a low-browed, beetling shop, below a penthouse roof, where iron, old rags, bottles, bones, and greasy offal were bought. Upon the floor within were piled up heaps of rusty keys, nails, chains, hinges, files, scales, weights, and refuse iron of all kinds. Secrets that few would like to scrutinize were bred and hidden in mountains of unseemly rags, masses of corrupted fat, and sepulchers of bones. Sitting in among the wares he dealt in, by a charcoal stove made of old bricks, was a grey-haired rascal, nearly seventy years of age, who had screened himself from the cold air without by a frowzy curtaining of miscellaneous tatters hung upon a line, and smoked his pipe in all the luxury of calm retirement.

Scrooge and the Phantom came into the presence of this man, just as a woman with a heavy bundle slunk into the shop. But she had scarcely entered, when another woman, similarly laden, came in too, and she was closely followed by a man in faded black, who was no less startled by the sight of them than they had been upon the recognition of each other. After a short period of blank astonishment, in which the old man with the pipe had joined them, they all three burst into a laugh.

"Let the charwoman[1] alone to be the first!" cried she who had entered first. "Let the laundress alone to be the second; and let the undertaker's man alone to be the third. Look here, old Joe, here's a chance! If we haven't all three met here without meaning it!"

---

[1] maid or housekeeper

"You couldn't have met in a better place," said old Joe, removing his pipe from his mouth. "Come into the parlor. You were made free of it long ago, you know; and the other two an't strangers. Stop till I shut the door of the shop. Ah! How it skreeks! There an't such a rusty bit of metal in the place as its own hinges, I believe; and I'm sure there's no such old bones here as mine. Ha! Ha! We're all suitable to our calling, we're well matched. Come into the parlor. Come into the parlor."

The parlor was the space behind the screen of rags. The old man raked the fire together with an old stair-rod, and, having trimmed his smoky lamp (for it was night) with the stem of his pipe, put it into his mouth again.

While he did this, the woman who had already spoken threw her bundle on the floor, and sat down in a flaunting manner on a stool; crossing her elbows on her knees, and looking with a bold defiance at the other two.

"What odds, then? What odds, Mrs. Dilber?" said the woman. "Every person has a right to take care of themselves. He always did!"

"That's true, indeed!" said the laundress. "No man more so."

"Why, then, don't stand staring as if you was afraid, woman! Who's the wiser? We're not going to pick holes in each other's coats, I suppose?"

"No, indeed!" said Mrs. Dilber and the man together. "We should hope not."

"Very well, then!" cried the woman. "That's enough. Who's the worse for the loss of a few things like these? Not a dead man, I suppose?"

"No, indeed," said Mrs. Dilber, laughing.

"If he wanted to keep 'em after he was dead, a wicked old screw," pursued the woman, "why wasn't he natural in his lifetime? If he had been, he'd have had somebody to look after him when he was struck with Death, instead of lying gasping out his last there, alone by himself."

"It's the truest word that ever was spoke," said Mrs. Dilber. "It's a judgment on him."

"I wish it was a little heavier judgment," replied the woman; "and it should have been, you may depend upon it, if I could have laid my hands on anything else. Open that bundle, old Joe, and let me know the value of it. Speak out plain. I'm not afraid to be the first, nor afraid for them to see it. We knew pretty well that we were helping ourselves before we met here, I believe. It's no sin. Open the bundle, Joe."

But the gallantry of her friends would not allow of this; and the man in faded black, mounting the breach first, produced his plunder. It was not extensive. A seal or two, a pencil-case, a pair of sleeve-buttons, and a brooch of no great value, were all. They were severally examined and appraised by old Joe, who chalked the sums he was disposed to give for each upon the wall, and added them up into a total when he found that there was nothing more to come.

"That's your account," said Joe, "and I wouldn't give another sixpence, if I was to be boiled for not doing it. Who's next?"

Mrs. Dilber was next. Sheets and towels, a little wearing apparel, two old-fashioned silver teaspoons, a pair of sugar tongs, and a few boots. Her account was stated on the wall in the same manner.

"I always give too much to ladies. It's a weakness of mine, and that's the way I ruin myself," said old Joe. "That's your account. If you asked me for another penny, and made it an open question, I'd repent of being so liberal, and knock off half a crown."

"And now undo my bundle, Joe," said the first woman.

Joe went down on his knees for the greater convenience of opening it, and, having unfastened a great many knots, dragged out a large heavy roll of some dark stuff.

"What do you call this?" said Joe. "Bed curtains?"

A CHRISTMAS CAROL

"Ah!" returned the woman, laughing and leaning forward on her crossed arms. "Bed curtains!"

"You don't mean to say you took 'em down, rings and all, with him lying there?" said Joe.

"Yes, I do," replied the woman. "Why not?"

"You were born to make your fortune," said Joe, "and you'll certainly do it."

"I certainly shan't hold my hand, when I can get anything in it by reaching it out, for the sake of such a man as He was, I promise you, Joe," returned the woman coolly. "Don't drop that oil upon the blankets, now."

"His blankets?" asked Joe.

"Whose else's do you think?" replied the woman. "He isn't likely to take cold without 'em, I dare say."

"I hope he didn't die of anything catching? Eh?" said old Joe, stopping in his work, and looking up.

"Don't you be afraid of that," returned the woman. "I an't so fond of his company that I'd loiter about him for such things, if he did. Ah! You may look through that shirt till your eyes ache; but you won't find a hole in it, nor a threadbare place. It's the best he had, and a fine one too. They'd have wasted it, if it hadn't been for me."

"What do you call wasting of it?" asked old Joe.

"Putting it on him to be buried in, to be sure," replied the woman with a laugh. "Somebody was fool enough to do it, but I took it off again. If calico an't good enough for such a purpose, it isn't good enough for anything. It's quite as becoming to the body. He can't look uglier than he did in that one."

Scrooge listened to this dialogue in horror. As they sat grouped about their spoil, in the scanty light afforded by the old man's lamp, he viewed them with a detestation and disgust which could hardly have been greater, though they had been obscene demons, marketing the corpse itself.

"Ha, ha!" laughed the same woman when old Joe, producing a flannel bag with money in it, told out their several gains upon the ground. "This is the end of it, you see! He frightened every one away from him when he was alive, to profit us when he was dead! Ha, ha, ha!"

"Spirit!" said Scrooge, shuddering from head to foot. "I see, I see. The case of this unhappy man might be my own. My life tends that way now. Merciful Heaven, what is this?"

And though after my skin worms destroy this body, yet in my flesh shall I see God (Job 19:26)

A CHRISTMAS CAROL

Discussion Question:
What legacy do you wish to leave behind?

December 21

E RECOILED IN TERROR, for the scene had changed, and now he almost touched a bed: a bare, uncurtained bed: on which, beneath a ragged sheet, there lay a something covered up, which, though it was dumb, announced itself in awful language.

The room was very dark, too dark to be observed with any accuracy, though Scrooge glanced round it in obedience to a secret impulse, anxious to know what kind of room it was. A pale light, rising in the outer air, fell straight upon the bed: and on it, plundered and bereft, unwatched, unwept, uncared for, was the body of this man.

Scrooge glanced towards the Phantom. Its steady hand was pointed to the head. The cover was so carelessly adjusted that the slightest raising of it, the motion of a finger upon Scrooge's part, would have disclosed the face.

He thought of it, felt how easy it would be to do, and longed to do it; but had no more power to withdraw the veil than to dismiss the specter at his side.

Oh, cold, cold, rigid, dreadful Death, set up thine altar here, and dress it with such terrors as thou hast at thy command: for this is thy dominion! But of the loved, revered, and honored head thou canst not turn one hair to thy dread purposes, or make one feature odious. It is not that the hand is heavy, and will fall down when released; it is not that the heart and pulse are still; but that the hand WAS open, generous, and true; the heart brave, warm, and tender; and the pulse a man's. Strike, Shadow, strike! And see his good deeds springing from the wound, to sow the world with life immortal!

No voice pronounced these words in Scrooge's ears, and yet he heard them when he looked upon the bed. He thought, if this man could be raised up now, what would be his foremost thoughts? Avarice, hard dealing, griping cares? They have brought him to a rich end, truly!

He lay, in the dark, empty house, with not a man, a woman, or a child to say he was kind to me in this or that, and for the memory of one kind word I will be kind to him. A cat was tearing at the door, and there was a sound of gnawing rats beneath the hearth-stone. What they wanted in the room of death, and why they were so restless and disturbed, Scrooge did not dare to think.

"Spirit!" he said, "this is a fearful place. In leaving it, I shall not leave its lesson, trust me. Let us go!"

Still the Ghost pointed with an unmoved finger to the head.

"I understand you," Scrooge returned, "and I would do it if I could. But I have not the power, Spirit. I have not the power."

Again it seemed to look upon him.

"If there is any person in the town who feels emotion caused by this man's death," said Scrooge, quite agonized, "show that person to me, Spirit! I beseech you."

The Phantom spread its dark robe before him for a moment, like a wing; and, withdrawing it, revealed a room by daylight, where a mother and her children were.

She was expecting someone, and with anxious eagerness; for she walked up and down the room; started at every sound; looked out from the window; glanced at the clock; tried, but in vain, to work with her needle; and could hardly bear the voices of her children in their play.

A CHRISTMAS CAROL

At length the long-expected knock was heard. She hurried to the door, and met her husband; a man whose face was careworn and depressed, though he was young. There was a remarkable expression in it now; a kind of serious delight of which he felt ashamed, and which he struggled to repress.

He sat down to the dinner that had been hoarding for him by the fire, and, when she asked him faintly what news (which was not until after a long silence), he appeared embarrassed how to answer.

"Is it good," she said, "or bad?" to help him.

"Bad," he answered.

"We are quite ruined?"

"No. There is hope yet, Caroline."

"If he relents," she said, amazed, "there is! Nothing is past hope, if such a miracle has happened."

"He is past relenting," said her husband. "He is dead."

She was a mild and patient creature, if her face spoke truth; but she was thankful in her soul to hear it, and she said so with clasped hands. She prayed forgiveness the next moment, and was sorry; but the first was the emotion of her heart.

"What the half-drunken woman, whom I told you of last night, said to me when I tried to see him and obtain a week's delay, and what I thought was a mere excuse to avoid me, turns out to have been quite true. He was not only very ill, but dying, then."

"To whom will our debt be transferred?"

"I don't know. But, before that time, we shall be ready with the money; and, even though we were not, it would be bad fortune indeed to find so merciless a creditor in his successor. We may sleep tonight with light hearts, Caroline!"

Yes. Soften it as they would, their hearts were lighter. The children's faces, hushed and clustered round to hear what they so little understood, were brighter; and it was a happier house for this man's death! The only emotion that the Ghost could show him, caused by the event, was one of pleasure.

"Let me see some tenderness connected with a death," said Scrooge; "or that dark chamber, Spirit, which we left just now, will be for ever present to me."

The Ghost conducted him through several streets familiar to his feet; and, as they went along, Scrooge looked here and there to find himself, but nowhere was he to be seen. They entered poor Bob Cratchit's house,—the dwelling he had visited before,—and found the mother and the children seated round the fire.

A CHRISTMAS CAROL

Quiet. Very quiet. The noisy little Cratchits were as still as statues in one corner, and sat looking up at Peter, who had a book before him. The mother and her daughters were engaged in sewing. But surely they were very quiet!

"'And he took a child, and set him in the midst of them.'"

Where had Scrooge heard those words? He had not dreamed them. The boy must have read them out, as he and the Spirit crossed the threshold. Why did he not go on?

The mother laid her work upon the table, and put her hand up to her face.

"The color hurts my eyes," she said.

The color? Ah, poor Tiny Tim!

"They're better now again," said Cratchit's wife. "It makes them weak by candlelight; and I wouldn't show weak eyes to your father, when he comes home, for the world. It must be near his time."

"Past it rather," Peter answered, shutting up his book. "But I think he has walked a little slower than he used, these few last evenings, mother."

They were very quiet again. At last she said, and in a steady, cheerful voice, that only faltered once: "I have known him walk with—I have known him walk with Tiny Tim upon his shoulder very fast indeed."

"And so have I," cried Peter. "Often."

"And so have I," exclaimed another. So had all.

"But he was very light to carry," she resumed, intent upon her work, "and his father loved him so, that it was no trouble: no trouble. And there is your father at the door!"

Whosoever shall receive one of such children in my name, receiveth me: and whosoever shall receive me, receiveth not me, but him that sent me. (Mark 9:37)

Discussion Question:
What good deeds can you sow that will live on after you?

December 22

SHE HURRIED OUT TO meet him; and little Bob in his comforter—he had need of it, poor fellow—came in. His tea was ready for him on the hob, and they all tried who should help him to it most. Then the two young Cratchits got upon his knees, and laid, each child, a little cheek against his face, as if they said, "Don't mind it, father. Don't be grieved!"

Bob was very cheerful with them, and spoke pleasantly to all the family. He looked at the work upon the table, and praised the industry and speed of Mrs. Cratchit and the girls. They would be done long before Sunday, he said.

"Sunday! You went today, then, Robert?" said his wife.

"Yes, my dear," returned Bob. "I wish you could have gone. It would have done you good to see how green a place it is. But you'll see it often. I promised him that I would walk there on a Sunday. My little, little child!" cried Bob. "My little child!"

He broke down all at once. He couldn't help it. If he could have helped it, he and his child would have been farther apart, perhaps, than they were.

He left the room, and went upstairs into the room above, which was lighted cheerfully, and hung with Christmas. There was a chair set close beside the child, and there were signs of some one having been there lately. Poor Bob sat down in it, and, when he had thought a little and composed himself, he kissed the little face. He was reconciled to what had happened, and went down again quite happy.

They drew about the fire, and talked; the girls and mother working still. Bob told them of the extraordinary kindness of Mr. Scrooge's nephew, whom he had scarcely seen but once, and who, meeting him in the street that day, and seeing that he looked a little—"just a little down, you know," said Bob, inquired what had happened to distress him. "On which," said Bob, "for he is the pleasantest-spoken gentleman you ever heard, I told him. 'I am heartily sorry for it, Mr. Cratchit,' he said, 'and heartily sorry for your good wife.' By-the-bye, how he ever knew that I don't know."

"Knew what, my dear?"

A CHRISTMAS CAROL

"Why, that you were a good wife," replied Bob.

"Everybody knows that," said Peter.

"Very well-observed, my boy!" cried Bob. "I hope they do. 'Heartily sorry,' he said, 'for your good wife. If I can be of service to you in any way,' he said, giving me his card, 'that's where I live. Pray come to me.' Now, it wasn't," cried Bob, "for the sake of anything he might be able to do for us, so much as for his kind way, that this was quite delightful. It really seemed as if he had known our Tiny Tim, and felt with us."

"I'm sure he's a good soul!" said Mrs. Cratchit.

"You would be sure of it, my dear," returned Bob, "if you saw and spoke to him. I shouldn't be at all surprised—mark what I say!—if he got Peter a better situation."

"Only hear that, Peter," said Mrs. Cratchit.

"And then," cried one of the girls, "Peter will be keeping company with someone, and setting up for himself."

"Get along with you!" retorted Peter, grinning.

"It's just as likely as not," said Bob, "one of these days; though there's plenty of time for that, my dear. But, however and whenever we part from one another, I am sure we shall none of us forget poor Tiny Tim—shall we—or this first parting that there was among us?"

"Never, father!" cried they all.

"And I know," said Bob, "I know, my dears, that when we recollect how patient and how mild he was, although he was a little, little child, we shall not quarrel easily among ourselves, and forget poor Tiny Tim in doing it."

"No, never, father!" they all cried again.

"I am very happy," said little Bob, "I am very happy!"

Mrs. Cratchit kissed him, his daughters kissed him, the two young Cratchits kissed him, and Peter and himself shook hands. Spirit of Tiny Tim, thy childish essence was from God!

"Specter," said Scrooge, "something informs me that our parting moment is at hand. I know it, but I know not how. Tell me what man that was whom we saw lying dead?"

The Ghost of Christmas Yet To Come conveyed him, as before—though at a different time, he thought: indeed, there seemed no order in these latter visions, save that they were in the Future—into the resorts of business men, but showed him not himself. Indeed, the Spirit did not stay for anything, but went straight on, as to the end just now desired, until besought by Scrooge to tarry for a moment.

A CHRISTMAS CAROL

"This court," said Scrooge, "through which we hurry now, is where my place of occupation is, and has been for a length of time. I see the house. Let me behold what I shall be in days to come."

The Spirit stopped; the hand was pointed elsewhere.

"The house is yonder," Scrooge exclaimed. "Why do you point away?"

The inexorable finger underwent no change.

Scrooge hastened to the window of his office, and looked in. It was an office still, but not his. The furniture was not the same, and the figure in the chair was not himself. The Phantom pointed as before.

He joined it once again, and, wondering why and whither he had gone, accompanied it until they reached an iron gate. He paused to look round before entering.

A churchyard. Here, then, the wretched man, whose name he had now to learn, lay underneath the ground. It was a worthy place. Walled in by houses; overrun by grass and weeds, the growth of vegetation's death, not life; choked up with too much burying; fat with repleted appetite. A worthy place!

The Spirit stood among the graves, and pointed down to One. He advanced towards it trembling. The Phantom was exactly as it had been, but he dreaded that he saw new meaning in its solemn shape.

"Before I draw nearer to that stone to which you point," said Scrooge, "answer me one question. Are these the shadows of the things that Will be, or are they shadows of the things that May be only?"

Still the Ghost pointed downward to the grave by which it stood.

"Men's courses will foreshadow certain ends, to which, if persevered in, they must lead," said Scrooge. "But if the courses be departed from, the ends will change. Say it is thus with what you show me!"

The Spirit was immovable as ever.

Scrooge crept towards it, trembling as he went; and, following the finger, read upon the stone of the neglected grave his own name, Ebenezer Scrooge.

"Am I that man who lay upon the bed?" he cried upon his knees.

The finger pointed from the grave to him, and back again.

"No, Spirit! Oh no, no!"

The finger still was there.

"Spirit!" he cried, tight clutching at its robe, "Hear me! I am not the man I was. I will not be the man I must have been but for this

A CHRISTMAS CAROL

intercourse. Why show me this, if I am past all hope?"

For the first time the hand appeared to shake.

"Good Spirit," he pursued, as down upon the ground he fell before it: "your nature intercedes for me, and pities me. Assure me that I yet may change these shadows you have shown me by an altered life?"

The kind hand trembled.

"I will honor Christmas in my heart, and try to keep it all the year. I will live in the Past, the Present, and the Future. The Spirits of all Three shall strive within me. I will not shut out the lessons that they teach. Oh, tell me I may sponge away the writing on this stone!"

In his agony, he caught the spectral hand. It sought to free itself, but he was strong in his entreaty, and detained it. The Spirit, stronger yet, repulsed him.

Holding up his hands in a last prayer to have his fate reversed, he saw an alteration in the Phantom's hood and dress. It shrunk, collapsed, and dwindled down into a bedpost.

And now abideth faith, hope, charity, these three; but the greatest of these is charity. (1 Corinthians 13:13)

CHARLES DICKENS

Discussion Question:
What have you learned from your consideration of your past, present, and future? What is your resolution?

December 23

YES! AND THE BEDPOST was his own. The bed was his own, the room was his own. Best and happiest of all, the Time before him was his own, to make amends in!

"I will live in the Past, the Present, and the Future!" Scrooge repeated as he scrambled out of bed. "The Spirits of all Three shall strive within me. Oh, Jacob Marley! Heaven and the Christmas Time be praised for this! I say it on my knees, old Jacob; on my knees!"

He was so fluttered and so glowing with his good intentions, that his broken voice would scarcely answer to his call. He had been sobbing violently in his conflict with the Spirit, and his face was wet with tears.

"They are not torn down," cried Scrooge, folding one of his bed curtains in his arms, "they are not torn down, rings and all. They are here—I am here—the shadows of the things that would have been may be dispelled. They will be. I know they will!"

His hands were busy with his garments all this time; turning them inside out, putting them on upside down, tearing them, mislaying them, making them parties to every kind of extravagance.

"I don't know what to do!" cried Scrooge, laughing and crying in the same breath; and making a perfect Laocoön of himself with his stockings.[1] "I am as light as a feather, I am as happy as an angel, I am as merry as a schoolboy. I am as giddy as a drunken man. A merry Christmas to everybody! A happy New Year to all the world! Hallo here! Whoop! Hallo!"

He had frisked into the sitting-room, and was now standing there: perfectly winded.

"There's the saucepan that the gruel was in!" cried Scrooge, starting off again, and going round the fireplace. "There's the door by which the Ghost of Jacob Marley entered! There's the corner where the Ghost of Christmas Present sat! There's the window where I saw the wandering Spirits! It's all right, it's all true, it all happened. Ha, ha, ha!"

---

[1] Naked like Michelangelo's statue of Laocoön, except for his socks.

A CHRISTMAS CAROL

Really, for a man who had been out of practice for so many years, it was a splendid laugh, a most illustrious laugh. The father of a long, long line of brilliant laughs!

"I don't know what day of the month it is," said Scrooge. "I don't know how long I have been among the Spirits. I don't know anything. I'm quite a baby. Never mind. I don't care. I'd rather be a baby. Hallo! Whoop! Hallo here!"

He was checked in his transports by the churches ringing out the lustiest peals he had ever heard. Clash, clash, hammer; ding, dong, bell! Bell, dong, ding; hammer, clang, clash! Oh, glorious, glorious!

Running to the window, he opened it, and put out his head. No fog, no mist; clear, bright, jovial, stirring, cold; cold, piping for the blood to dance to; Golden sunlight; Heavenly sky; sweet fresh air; merry bells. Oh, glorious! Glorious!

"What's today?" cried Scrooge, calling downward to a boy in Sunday clothes, who perhaps had loitered in to look about him.

"Eh?" returned the boy with all his might of wonder.

"What's today, my fine fellow?" said Scrooge.

"Today!" replied the boy. "Why, Christmas Day."

"It's Christmas Day!" said Scrooge to himself. "I haven't missed it. The Spirits have done it all in one night. They can do anything they like. Of course they can. Of course they can. Hallo, my fine fellow!"

"Hallo!" returned the boy.

"Do you know the Poulterer's in the next street but one, at the corner?" Scrooge inquired.

"I should hope I did," replied the lad.

"An intelligent boy!" said Scrooge. "A remarkable boy! Do you know whether they've sold the prize Turkey that was hanging up there?—Not the little prize Turkey: the big one?"

"What! The one as big as me?" returned the boy.

"What a delightful boy!" said Scrooge. "It's a pleasure to talk to him. Yes, my buck!"

"It's hanging there now," replied the boy.

"Is it?" said Scrooge. "Go and buy it."

"Walk-er!"[1] exclaimed the boy.

"No, no," said Scrooge, "I am in earnest. Go and buy it, and tell 'em to bring it here, that I may give them the directions where to take it. Come back with the man, and I'll give you a

---

[1] Are you pulling my leg? From 'Hookey Walker,' a man whose reports were not to be believed.

A CHRISTMAS CAROL

shilling. Come back with him in less than five minutes, and I'll give you half a crown!"

The boy was off like a shot. He must have had a steady hand at a trigger who could have got a shot off half so fast.

"I'll send it to Bob Cratchit's," whispered Scrooge, rubbing his hands, and splitting with a laugh. "He shan't know who sends it. It's twice the size of Tiny Tim. Joe Miller never made such a joke as sending it to Bob's will be!"

The hand in which he wrote the address was not a steady one; but write it he did, somehow, and went downstairs to open the street door, ready for the coming of the poulterer's man. As he stood there, waiting his arrival, the knocker caught his eye.

"I shall love it as long as I live!" cried Scrooge, patting it with his hand. "I scarcely ever looked at it before. What an honest expression it has in its face! It's a wonderful knocker!—Here's the Turkey. Hallo! Whoop! How are you? Merry Christmas!"

It was a Turkey! He never could have stood upon his legs, that bird. He would have snapped 'em short off in a minute, like sticks of sealing wax.

"Why, it's impossible to carry that to Camden Town," said Scrooge. "You must have a cab."

CHARLES DICKENS

The chuckle with which he said this, and the chuckle with which he paid for the Turkey, and the chuckle with which he paid for the cab, and the chuckle with which he recompensed the boy, were only to be exceeded by the chuckle with which he sat down breathless in his chair again, and chuckled till he cried.

By pureness, by knowledge, by longsuffering, by kindness, by the Holy Ghost, by love unfeigned (2 Corinthians 6:6)

Discussion Question:
What service can you do for another this Christmas?

December 24

SHAVING WAS NOT AN easy task, for his hand continued to shake very much; and shaving requires attention, even when you don't dance while you are at it. But, if he had cut the end of his nose off, he would have put a piece of sticking-plaster over it, and been quite satisfied.

He dressed himself "all in his best," and at last got out into the streets. The people were by this time pouring forth, as he had seen them with the Ghost of Christmas Present; and, walking with his hands behind him, Scrooge regarded every one with a delighted smile. He looked so irresistibly pleasant, in a word, that three or four good-humored fellows said, "Good morning, sir! A merry Christmas to you!" And Scrooge said often afterward that, of all the blithe sounds he had ever heard, those were the blithest in his ears.

He had not gone far when, coming on towards him, he beheld the portly gentleman who had walked into his counting house the day before, and said, "Scrooge and Marley's, I believe?" It sent a pang across his heart to think how this old gentleman would look upon him when they met; but he knew what path lay straight before him, and he took it.

"My dear sir," said Scrooge, quickening his pace, and taking the old gentleman by both his hands, "how do you do? I hope you succeeded yesterday. It was very kind of you. A merry Christmas to you, sir!"

"Mr. Scrooge?"

"Yes," said Scrooge. "That is my name, and I fear it may not be pleasant to you. Allow me to ask your pardon. And will you have the goodness—" Here Scrooge whispered in his ear.

"Lord bless me!" cried the gentleman, as if his breath were taken away. "My dear Mr. Scrooge, are you serious?"

"If you please," said Scrooge. "Not a farthing less. A great many back-payments are included in it, I assure you. Will you do me that favor?"

"My dear sir," said the other, shaking hands with him, "I don't know what to say to such munifi—"[1]

"Don't say anything, please," retorted Scrooge. "Come and see me. Will you come and see me?"

"I will!" cried the old gentleman. And it was clear he meant to do it.

"Thankee," said Scrooge. "I am much obliged to you. I thank you fifty times. Bless you!"

He went to church, and walked about the streets, and watched the people hurrying to and fro, and patted the children on the head, and questioned beggars, and looked down into the kitchens of houses, and up to the windows; and found that everything could yield him pleasure. He had never dreamed that any walk—that anything—could give him so much happiness. In the afternoon he turned his steps towards his nephew's house.

He passed the door a dozen times before he had the courage to go up and knock. But he made a dash, and did it.

"Is your master at home, my dear?" said Scrooge to the girl. Nice girl! Very.

"Yes sir."

---

[1] munificence

"Where is he, my love?" said Scrooge.

"He's in the dining room, sir, along with mistress. I'll show you upstairs, if you please."

"Thankee. He knows me," said Scrooge, with his hand already on the dining room lock. "I'll go in here, my dear."

He turned it gently, and sidled his face in round the door. They were looking at the table (which was spread out in great array); for these young housekeepers are always nervous on such points, and like to see that everything is right.

"Fred!" said Scrooge.

Dear heart alive, how his niece by marriage started! Scrooge had forgotten, for the moment, about her sitting in the corner with the footstool, or he wouldn't have done it on any account.

"Why, bless my soul!" cried Fred, "Who's that?"

"It's I. Your uncle Scrooge. I have come to dinner. Will you let me in, Fred?"

Let him in! It is a mercy he didn't shake his arm off. He was at home in five minutes. Nothing could be heartier. His niece looked just the same. So did Topper when he came. So did the plump sister when she came. So did everyone when they came. Wonderful party,

A CHRISTMAS CAROL

wonderful games, wonderful unanimity, wonderful happiness!

But he was early at the office next morning. Oh, he was early there! If he could only be there first, and catch Bob Cratchit coming late! That was the thing he had set his heart upon.

And he did it; yes, he did! The clock struck nine. No Bob. A quarter past. No Bob. He was full eighteen minutes and a half behind his time. Scrooge sat with his door wide open, that he might see him come into the tank.

His hat was off before he opened the door; his comforter too. He was on his stool in a jiffy; driving away with his pen, as if he were trying to overtake nine o'clock.

"Hallo!" growled Scrooge in his accustomed voice as near as he could feign it. "What do you mean by coming here at this time of day?"

"I am very sorry, sir," said Bob. "I am behind my time."

"You are!" repeated Scrooge. "Yes. I think you are. Step this way, sir, if you please."

"It's only once a year, sir," pleaded Bob, appearing from the tank. "It shall not be repeated. I was making rather merry yesterday, sir."

"Now, I'll tell you what, my friend," said Scrooge. "I am not going to stand this sort of thing any longer. And therefore," he continued, leaping from his stool, and giving Bob such a dig in the waistcoat that he staggered back into the tank again: "and therefore I am about to raise your salary!"

Bob trembled, and got a little nearer to the ruler. He had a momentary idea of knocking Scrooge down with it, holding him, and calling to the people in the court for help and a strait-waistcoat.[1]

"A merry Christmas, Bob!" said Scrooge with an earnestness that could not be mistaken, as he clapped him on the back. "A merrier Christmas, Bob, my good fellow, than I have given you for many a year! I'll raise your salary, and endeavor to assist your struggling family, and we will discuss your affairs this very afternoon, over a Christmas bowl of smoking bishop,[2] Bob! Make up the fires and buy another coal-scuttle before you dot another i, Bob Cratchit!"

Scrooge was better than his word. He did it all, and infinitely more; and to Tiny Tim, who did NOT die, he was a second father. He became as good a friend, as good a master, and as good a man as the good old City knew, or

---

[1] Straitjacket, to restrain a crazy man.
[2] mulled wine/wassail

any other good old city, town, or borough in the good old world. Some people laughed to see the alteration in him, but he let them laugh, and little heeded them; for he was wise enough to know that nothing ever happened on this globe, for good, at which some people did not have their fill of laughter in the outset; and, knowing that such as these would be blind anyway, he thought it quite as well that they should wrinkle up their eyes in grins as have the malady in less attractive forms. His own heart laughed: and that was quite enough for him.

He had no further intercourse with Spirits, but lived upon the Total-Abstinence Principle[1] ever afterwards; and it was always said of him that he knew how to keep Christmas well, if any man alive possessed the knowledge. May that be truly said of us, and all of us! And so, as Tiny Tim observed, God Bless Us, Every One!

Charity suffereth long, and is kind; charity envieth not; charity vaunteth not itself, is not puffed up, doth not behave itself unseemly, seeketh not her own, is not easily provoked, thinketh no evil; rejoiceth not in iniquity, but rejoiceth in the truth; beareth all things, believeth all things, hopeth all things, endureth all things. Charity never faileth: but whether

---

[1] Refraining from being bitter, mean-spirited, angry, dour, greedy, grasping, self-centered, and unforgiving.

CHARLES DICKENS

there be prophecies, they shall fail; whether there be tongues, they shall cease; whether there be knowledge, it shall vanish away. (1 Corinthians 13:4-8)

Discussion Question:
How are you doing at living by the Total Abstinence Principle?

Extension activities

Here are a few extension activities that you can try, to get your juices flowing. Feel free to add your own ideas!

- Watch and compare various versions (plays/movies) of The Christmas Carol
- Act out your own version
- Create a diorama or costume
- Write a sequel
- Write a modern take or put The Christmas Carol in another setting
- Write a list of things that you can do to show kindness to others this Christmas
- Charles Dickens' use of commas is quite different from modern American usage. Copy a paragraph from The Christmas Carol and standardize the comma usage.
- Compare and contrast your Christmas traditions with those of Scrooge or Cratchit?

The Life of Our Lord

Special 24-Day Advent Reader

Charles Dickens

Foreword

Charles Dickens wrote this delightful little book in 1849 for his most private and personal readership—his own children. With no eye on publicity or pandering to any faction of his vast following, we can see here his own thoughts on the Christian Religion distilled, not only for the benefit of young readers but almost, one feels, to repeat to himself his belief in the Good News of God, and tell again the Gospel story in a pleasantly simple yet direct ad accurate way.

This brings a message of its own which should be important to all families of the world. Today I want to add to it a deeper understanding of who Jesus Christ was and still remains. He is, for most of us, God-made-man for our salvation, born of the Virgin Mary, and with Joseph as his chosen earthly foster father. We should strive to understand even more fully the Salvation Jesus achieved for us and how it happened and continues to happen in the Holy Eucharist, and in the life of Christ's Church throughout the world.

Though Charles Dickens had refused publication of this book during his own lifetime or that of his children, one of his sons, my great-grandfather Sir Henry Fielding Dickens set down in his Will that at his death the book might be released with the full consent of the family. This was granted and the work was published in 1934.

I, my wife Jeanne-Marie and daughters Catherine and Lucy hope that reading this book will be a very special little spiritual exercise, and that the sincerity of the message may lead us all towards a better understanding of God.

Christopher Charles Dickens, March 1996

December 1

Y DEAR CHILDREN, I am very anxious that you should know something about the History of Jesus Christ. For everybody ought to know about Him. No one ever lived, who was so good, so kind, so gentle, and so sorry for all people who did wrong, or were in any way ill or miserable, as he was. And as he is now in Heaven, where we hope to go, and all to meet each other after we are dead, and there be happy always together, you never can think what a good place Heaven, is without knowing who he was and what he did.

He was born, a long long time ago—nearly Two Thousand years ago—at a place called Bethlehem. His father and mother lived in a city called Nazareth, but they were forced, by business to travel to Bethlehem.[32] His father's

---

[32] For a census ordered by Rome

THE LIFE OF OUR LORD

name was Joseph, and his mother's name was Mary.

And the town being very full of people, also brought there by business, there was no room for Joseph and Mary in the Inn or any house; so they went into a Stable to lodge, and in this stable Jesus Christ was born. There was no cradle or anything of that kind there, so Mary laid her pretty little boy in what is called the Manger, which is the place the horses eat out of. And there he fell asleep.

While he was asleep, some Shepherds who were watching Sheep in the Fields, saw an Angel from God, all light and beautiful, come moving over the grass towards them. At first they were afraid and fell down and hid their faces. But it said "There is a child born today in the city of Bethlehem near here, who will grow up to be so good that God will love him as his own son; and he will teach men to love one another, and not to quarrel and hurt one another; and his name will be Jesus Christ; and people will put that name in their prayers, because they will know God loves it, and will know that they should love it too." And then the Angel told the Shepherds to go to that Stable, and look at that little child in the Manger. Which they did; and they kneeled down by it in its sleep, and said "God bless this child!"

Now the great place of all that country was Jerusalem—just as London is the great place in England—and at Jerusalem the King lived, whose name was King Herod. Some wise men came one day, from a country a long way off in the East, and said to the King "We have seen a Star in the Sky, which teaches us to know that a child is born in Bethlehem who will live to be a man whom all people will love." When King Herod heard this, he was jealous, for he was a wicked man. But he pretended not to be, and said to the wise men, "Whereabouts is this child?" And the wise men said "We don't know. But we think the Star will shew us; for the Star has been moving on before us, all the way here, and is now standing still in the sky." Then Herod asked them to see if the Star would shew them where the child lived, and ordered them, if they found the child, to come back to him. So they went out, and the Star went on, over their heads a little way before them, until it stopped over the house where the child was. This was very wonderful, but God ordered it to be so.

When the Star stopped, the wise men went in, and saw the child with Mary his Mother. They loved him very much, and gave him some presents. Then they went away. But they did not go back to King Herod; for they thought he was jealous, though he had not said so. So they went away, by night, back into their own country. And an Angel came, and told Joseph and Mary to take the child into a Country called Egypt, or Herod would kill him. So they escaped too, in the night—the father, the mother, and the child—and arrived there, safely.

But when this cruel Herod found that the wise men did not come back to him, and that he could not, therefore, find out where this child, Jesus Christ, lived, he called his soldiers and captains to him, and told them to go and Kill all the children in his dominions that were not more than two years old. The wicked men did so. The mothers of the children ran up and down the streets with them in their arms trying to save them, and hide them in caves and cellars, but it was of no use. The soldiers with their swords killed all the children they could find. This dreadful murder was called the Murder of the Innocents. Because the little children were so innocent.

King Herod hoped that Jesus Christ was one of them. But He was not, as you know, for He had escaped safely into Egypt. And he lived there, with his father and mother, until Bad King Herod died.

For unto you is born this day in the city of David a Saviour, which is Christ the Lord. (Luke 2:11)

Discussion Question:
Why is it so important for us to learn about Jesus Christ?

December 2

WHEN KING HEROD WAS dead, an angel came to Joseph again, and said he might now go to Jerusalem, and not be afraid for the child's sake. So Joseph and Mary, and her Son Jesus Christ (who are commonly called The Holy Family) travelled towards Jerusalem; but hearing on the way that King Herod's son was the new King, and fearing that he, too, might want to hurt the child, they turned out of the way, and went to live in Nazareth. They lived there, until Jesus Christ was twelve years old.

Then Joseph and Mary went to Jerusalem to attend a Religious Feast which used to be held in those days, in the Temple of Jerusalem, which was a great church or Cathedral; and they took Jesus Christ with them. And when the Feast was over, they travelled away from Jerusalem, back towards their own home in

Nazareth, with a great many of their friends and neighbors. For people used, then, to travel a great many together, for fear of robbers; the roads not being so safe and well-guarded as they are now, and traveling being much more difficult altogether, than it now is.

They travelled on. For a whole day, and never knew that Jesus Christ was not with them; for the company being so large, they thought he was somewhere among the people, though they did not see Him. But finding that he was not there, and fearing that he was lost, they turned back to Jerusalem in great anxiety to look for him. They found him, sitting in the temple, talking about the goodness of God, and how we should all pay to him, with some learned men who were called Doctors. They were not what you understand by the word "doctors" now; they did not attend sick people; they were scholars and clever men. And Jesus Christ shewed such knowledge in what said to them, and in the questions he asked them that they were all astonished.

He went, with Joseph and Mary, home to Nazareth, when they found him, and lived there until he was thirty or thirty-five years old.

THE LIFE OF OUR LORD

And he said unto them, How is it that ye sought me? wist ye not that I must be about my Father's business? (Luke 2:49)

Discussion Question:
How can we spread the word of God and glorify him?

December 3

AT THE TIME THERE was a very good man indeed, named John, who was the son of a woman named Elizabeth—the cousin of Mary. And people being wicked, and violent, and killing each other, and not minding their duty towards God, John (to teach them better) went about the country, preaching to them, and entreating them to be better men and women. And because he loved them more than himself, and didn't mind himself when he was doing them good, he was poorly dressed in the skin of a camel, and ate little but some insects called locusts, which he found as he travelled: and wild honey, which the bees left in the Hollow Trees.

You never saw a locust, because they belong to that country near Jerusalem, which is a great way off. So do camels, but I think you have seen a camel? At all events they are brought

THE LIFE OF OUR LORD

over here, sometimes; and if you would like to see one, I will shew you one.

There was a River, not very far from Jerusalem, called the River Jordan; and in this water, John baptized those people who would come to him, and promise to be better. A great many people went to him in crowds. Jesus Christ went too. But when John saw him, John said, "Why should I baptize you, who are so much better than me!" Jesus Christ made answer, "Suffer it to be so now." So John baptized him. And when he was baptized, the sky opened, and a beautiful bird like a dove came flying down, and the voice of God, speaking up in Heaven, was heard to say "This is my beloved Son, in whom I am well pleased!"

Jesus Christ then went into a wild and lovely country called the Wilderness, and stayed there forty days and forty nights, praying that he night be of use to men and women, and teach them to be better, so that after their deaths, they might be happy in Heaven.

When he came out of the Wilderness, he began to cure sick people by only laying his hand upon them; for God had given him power to heal the sick, and to give sight to the blind, and to do many wonderful and solemn things of which I shall tell you more by and by, and which are called "The Miracles" of Christ. I wish you would remember that word, because I shall use it again, and I should like you to know that it means something which is very wonderful and which could not be done without God's leave and assistance.

The first miracle which Jesus Christ did, was at a place called Cana, where he went to a Marriage Feast with Mary his Mother. There was not wine; and Mary told him so. There were only six stone water-pots filled with water. But Jesus turned this water into wine, by only lifting up his hand; and all who were there, drank of it.

For God had given Jesus Christ the power to do such wonders; and he did them, that people might know he was not a common man, and might believe what he taught them, and also believe that God had sent him. And many people, hearing this, and hearing that he cured the sick, did begin to believe in him; and great crowds followed him in the streets and on the roads, wherever he went.

And the Holy Ghost descended in a bodily shape like a dove upon him, and a voice came from heaven, which said, Thou art my beloved Son; in thee I am well pleased. (Luke 3:22)

THE LIFE OF OUR LORD

Discussion Question:
Why was Jesus baptized? Why should we be baptized?

December 4

THAT THERE MIGHT BE some good men to go about with Him, teaching the people, Jesus Christ chose Twelve poor men to be his companions. These twelve are called The Apostles or Disciples, and he chose them from among Poor Men, in order that the Poor might know—always after that; in all years to come—that Heaven was made for them as well as for the rich, and that God makes no difference between those who wear good clothes and those who go barefoot and in rags. The most miserable, the most ugly, deformed, wretched creatures that live, will be bright Angels in Heaven if they are good here on earth. Never forget this, when you are grown up. Never be proud or unkind, my dears, to any poor man, woman, or child. If they are bad, think that they would have been better, if they had had kind friends, and good homes, and had been better

THE LIFE OF OUR LORD

taught. So, always try to make them better by kind persuading words; and always try to teach them and relieve them if you can. And when people speak ill of the Poor and Miserable, think how Jesus Christ went among them and taught them, and thought them worthy of his care. And always pity them yourselves, and think as well of them as you can.

The names of the Twelve Apostles were, Simon Peter, Andrew, James the son of Zebedee, John, Philip, Bartholomew, Thomas, Matthew, James the son Alphaeus, Labbaeus, Simon, and Judas Iscariot. This man afterward betrayed Jesus Christ, as you will hear by and by.

The first four of these, were poor fishermen, who were sitting in their boats by the seaside, mending their nets, when Christ passed by. He stopped, and went into Simon Peter's boat, and asked him if he had caught many fish. Peter said No; though they had worked all night with their nets, they had caught nothing. Christ said, "Let down the net again." They did so; and it was immediately so full of fish, that it required the strength of many men (who came and helped them) to lift it out of the water, and even then it was very hard to do. This was another of the miracles of Jesus Christ.

Jesus then said, "Come with me." And they followed him directly. And from that time the Twelve disciples or apostles were always with him.

As great crowds of people followed him, and wished to be taught, he went up into a Mountain and there preached to them, and gave them, from his own lips, the words of that Prayer, beginning "Our Father which art in Heaven," that you say every night.[33] It is called The Lord's Prayer, because it was first said by Jesus Christ, and because he commanded his disciples to pray in those words.

---

[33] Our Father, which art in heaven,
Hallowed be thy Name.
Thy Kingdom come.
Thy will be done in earth,
As it is in heaven.
Give us this day our daily bread.
And forgive us our trespasses,
As we forgive them that trespass against us.
And lead us not into temptation,
But deliver us from evil.
For thine is the kingdom,
The power, and the glory,
For ever and ever.
Amen.

THE LIFE OF OUR LORD

When he was come down from the Mountain, there came to him a man with a dreadful disease called the leprosy. It was common in those times, and those who were ill with it, were called lepers. This Leper fell at the feet of Jesus Christ, and said "Lord! If thou wilt, thou canst make me well!" Jesus, always full of compassion, stretched out his hand, and said "I will! Be thou well!" And his disease went away, immediately, and he was cured.

And Jesus said unto them, Come ye after me, and I will make you to become fishers of men. (Mark 1:17)

Discussion Question:
How can we be like Jesus and relieve the poor and suffering?

December 5

BEING FOLLOWED, WHEREVER HE went, by great crowds of people, Jesus went, with his disciples, into a house, to rest. While he was sitting inside, some men brought upon a bed, a man who was very ill of what is called the Palsy, so that he trembled all over from head to foot, and could neither stand, nor move. But the crowd being all about the door and windows, and they not being able to get near Jesus Christ, these men climbed up to the roof of the house, which was a low one; and through the tiling at the top, let down the bed, with the sick man upon it, into the room where Jesus sat. When he saw him, Jesus, full of pity, said "Arise! Take up thy bed, and go to thine own home!" And the man rose up and went away quite well; blessing him, and thanking God.

THE LIFE OF OUR LORD

There was a Centurion too, or officer over the Soldiers, who came to him, and said, "Lord! My servant lies at home in my house, very ill."—Jesus Christ made answer, "I will come and cure him." But the Centurion said "Lord! I am not worthy that Thou shouldst come to my house. Say the word only, and I know he will be cured." Then Jesus Christ, glad that the Centurion believed in him so truly said "Be it so!" And the servant became well, from that moment.

But of all the people who came to him, none were so full of grief and distress, as one man who was a Ruler or Magistrate over many people, and he wrung his hands, and cried, and said "Oh Lord, my daughter—my beautiful, good, innocent little girl, is dead! Oh come to her, come to her, and lay Thy blessed hand upon her, and I know she will revive, and come to life again, and make me and her mother happy. Oh Lord we love her so, we love her so! And she is dead!"

Jesus Christ went out with him, and so did his disciples and went to his house, where the friends and neighbors were crying in the room where the poor dead little girl lay, and where there was soft music playing; as there used to be, in those days, when people died. Jesus Christ, looking on her, sorrowfully, said—to comfort her poor parents—"She is not dead. She is asleep." Then he commanded the room to be cleared of the people that were in it, and going to the dead child, took her by the hand, and she rose up, quite well, as if she had only been asleep. Oh what a sight it must have been to see her parents clasp her in their arms, and kiss her, and thank God, and Jesus Christ his son, for such great Mercy!

But he was always merciful and tender. And because he did such Good, and taught people how to love God and how to hope to go to Heaven after death, he was called Our Savior.

Wherefore neither thought I myself worthy to come unto thee: but say in a word, and my servant shall be healed. (Luke 7:7)

Discussion Question:
How can we show Jesus our faith?

December 6

THERE WERE IN THAT, country where Our Savior performed his Miracles, certain people who were called Pharisees. They were very proud, and believed that no people were good but themselves; and they were all afraid of Jesus Christ, because he taught the people better. So were the Jews, in general. Most of the Inhabitants of that country, were Jews.

Our Savior, walking once in the fields with his disciples on a Sunday (which the Jews called, and still call, the Sabbath) they gathered some ears of the corn that was growing there, to eat. This, the Pharisees said, was wrong; and in the same way, when our Savior went into one of their churches—they were called Synagogues—and looked compassionately on a poor man who had his hand all withered and wasted away, these Pharisees said "Is it right to cure people on a Sunday?" Our Savior answered them by saying, "If any of you had a sheep and it fell into a pit, would you not take it out, even though it happened on a Sunday? And how much better is a man than a sheep!" Then he said to the poor man, "Stretch out thine hand!" And it was cured immediately, and was smooth and useful like the other. So Jesus Christ told them "You may always do good, no matter what the day is."

There was a city called Nain into which Our Savior went soon after this, followed by great numbers of people, and especially by those who had sick relations, or friends, or children. For they brought sick people out into the streets and roads through which he passed, and cried out to him to touch them, and when he did, they became well. Going on, in the midst of this crowd, and near the Gate of the city, He met a funeral. It was the funeral of a young man, who was carried on what is called a Bier, which was open, as the custom was in that country, and is now in many parts of Italy. His poor mother followed the bier, and wept very much, for she had no other child. When Our Savior saw her, he was touched to the heart to see her so sorry and said "Weep not!" Then, the bearers of the bier standing still, he walked up to it and touched it with his hand, and said

"Young Man! Arise." The dead man, coming to life again at the sound of The Savior's Voice, rose up and began to speak. And Jesus Christ leaving him with his mother—Ah how happy they both were!—went away.

And he came and touched the bier: and they that bare him stood still. And he said, Young man, I say unto thee, Arise. (Luke 7:14)

Discussion Question:
How can we do good on the Sabbath?

December 7

BY THIS TIME THE crowd was so very great that Jesus Christ went down to the waterside, to go in a boat, to a more retired place. And in the boat, He fell asleep, while his Disciples were sitting on the deck. While he was still sleeping a violent storm arose, so that the waves washed over the boat, and the howling wind so rocked and shook it, that they thought it would sink. In their fright the disciples awoke Our Savior, and said "Lord! Save us, or we are lost!" He stood up, and raising his arm, said to the rolling Sea and to the whistling wind, "Peace! Be still!" And immediately it was calm and pleasant weather, and the boat went safely on, through the smooth waters.

When they came to the other side of the waters they had to pass a wild and lonely burying ground that was outside the City to

THE LIFE OF OUR LORD

which they were going. All burying grounds were outside cities in those times. In this place there was a dreadful madman who lived among the tombs, and howled all day and night, so that it made travelers afraid, to hear him.

They had tried to chain him, but he broke his chains, he was so strong; and he would throw himself on the sharp stones, and cut himself in the most dreadful manner; crying and howling all the while; When this wretched man saw Jesus Christ a long way off, he cried out "It is the son of God! Oh son of God, do not torment me!" Jesus, coming near him, perceived that he was torn by an Evil Spirit, and cast the madness out of him, and into a herd of swine (or pigs) who were feeding close by, and who directly ran headlong down a steep place leading to the sea and were dashed to pieces.

Now Herod, the son of that cruel King who murdered the Innocents, reigning over the people there, and hearing that Jesus Christ was doing these wonders, and was giving sight to the blind and causing the deaf to hear, and the dumb to speak, and the lame to walk, and that he was followed by multitudes and multitudes of people—Herod, hearing this, said "This man is a companion and friend of John the Baptist." John was the good man, you recollect, who wore a garment made of camel's hair, and ate wild honey. Herod had taken him Prisoner, because he taught and preached to the people; and had him then, locked up, in the prisons of his Palace.

While Herod was in this angry humor with John, his birthday came; and his daughter, Herodias, who was a fine dancer, danced before him, to please him. She pleased him so much that he swore on oath he would give her whatever she would ask him for. "Then," said she, "father, give me the head of John the Baptist in a charger." For she hated John, and was a wicked, cruel woman.

The King was sorry, for though he had John prisoner, he did not wish to kill him, but having sworn that he would give her what she asked for, he sent some soldiers down into the Prison, with directions to cut off the head of John the Baptist, and give it to Herodias. This they did, and took it to her, as she had said, in a charger, which was a kind of dish. When Jesus Christ heard from the apostles of this cruel deed, he left that city, and went with them (after they had privately buried John's body in the night) to another place.

And he arose, and rebuked the wind, and said unto the sea, Peace, be still. And the wind ceased, and there was a great calm. (Mark 4:39)

THE LIFE OF OUR LORD

Discussion Question:
What miracles has Jesus performed in your life? What is he capable of doing?

December 8

ONE OF THE PHARISEES begged Our Savior to go into his house, and eat with him. And while our Savior sat eating at the table, there crept into the room a woman of that city who had led a bad and sinful life, and was ashamed that the Son of God should see her; and yet she trusted so much to his goodness, and his compassion for all who, having done wrong were truly sorry for it in their hearts, that, by little and little she went behind the seat on which he sat, and dropped down at his feet, and wetted them with her sorrowful tears, then she kissed them and dried them on her long hair, and rubbed them with some sweet-smelling ointment she had brought with her in a box. Her name was Mary Magdalene.

When the Pharisee saw that Jesus permitted this woman to touch Him, he said within

THE LIFE OF OUR LORD

himself that Jesus did not know how wicked she had been. But Jesus Christ, who knew his thoughts, said to him "Simon"—for that was his name—"if a man had debtors, one of whom owed him five hundred pence, and one of whom owed him only fifty pence, and he forgave them, both, their debts, which of those two debtors do you think would love him most?" Simon answered "I suppose that one whom he forgave most." Jesus told him he was right, and said "As God forgives this woman so much sin, she will love Him, I hope, the more." And he said to her, "God forgives you!" The company who were present wondered that Jesus Christ had power to forgive sins, but God had given it to Him. And the woman thanking Him for all his mercy, went away.

We learn from this, this we must always forgive those who have done us any harm, when they come to us and say they are truly sorry for it. Even if they do not come and say so, we must still forgive them, and never hate them or be unkind to them, if we would hope that God will forgive us.

After this, there was a great feast of the Jews, and Jesus Christ went to Jerusalem. There was, near the sheep market in that place, a pool, or pond, called Bethesda, having five gates to it; and at the time of the year when that feast took place great numbers of sick people and cripples went to this pool to bathe in it; believing that an Angel came and stirred the water, and that whoever went in first after the Angel had done so, was cured of any illness he or she had, whatever it might be. Among these poor persons, was one man who had been ill, thirty-eight years; and he told Jesus Christ (who took pity on him when he saw him lying on his bed alone, with no one to help him) that he never could be dipped in the pool, because he was so weak and ill that he could not move to get there. Out Savior said to him, "take up thy bed and go away." And he went away, quite well.

Many Jews saw this; and when they saw it, they hated Jesus Christ the more; knowing that the people, being taught and cured by him, would not believe their Priests, who told the people what was not true, and deceived them. So they said to one another that Jesus Christ should be killed, because he cured people on the Sabbath Day (which was against their strict law) and because he called himself the Son of God. And they tried to raise enemies against him, and to get the crowd in the streets to murder Him.

Judge not, that ye be not judged. For with what judgment ye judge, ye shall be judged: and with what

measure ye mete, it shall be measured to you again.
(Matthew 7:1-2)

Discussion Question:
Who has wronged you the most? Have you tried to forgive them?

December 9

BUT THE CROWD FOLLOWED Him wherever he went, blessing him, and praying to be taught and cured; for they knew He did nothing but Good. Jesus going with his disciples over a sea, called the Sea of Tiberia and sitting with them on a hillside, saw great numbers of these poor people waiting below, and said to the apostle Philip. "Where shall we buy bread, that they may eat and be refreshed, after their long journey?" Philip answered, "Lord, two hundred penny-worthy of bread would not be enough for so many people, and we have none." "We have only," said another apostle—Andrew, Simon, Peter's brother—"five small barley loaves, and two little fish, belonging to a lad who is among us. What are they, among so many!" Jesus Christ said, "Let them all sit down!" They did; there being a great deal of grass in that place. When they were all seated, Jesus took the bread, and looked up to Heaven, and blessed it, and broke it, and handed it in pieces to the apostles, who handed it to the people. And of those five little loaves, and two fish, five thousand men, besides women, and children, ate, and had enough; and when they were all satisfied, there were gathered up twelve baskets full of what was left. This was another of the Miracles of Jesus Christ.

Our Savior then sent his disciples away in a boat, across the water, and said he would follow them presently, when he had dismissed the people. The people being gone, he remained by himself to pray; so that the night came on, and the disciples were still rowing on the water in their boat, wondering when Christ would come. Late in the night, when the wind was against them and the waves were running high, they saw Him coming walking towards them on the water, as if it were dry land. When they saw this, they were terrified, and cried out, but Jesus said, "It is I, Be not afraid!" Peter taking courage, said, "Lord, if it be thou, tell me to come to thee upon the water." Jesus Christ said, "Come!" Peter then walked towards Him, but seeing the angry waves, and hearing the wind roar, he was frightened and began to sink, and would have done so, but that Jesus took him by the hand, and let him into the boat. Then, in a moment, the wind went down; and the Disciples said to one another, "It is true! He is the Son of God!"

Jesus did many more miracles after this happened and cured the sick in great numbers; making the lame walk, and the dumb speak, and the blind see. And being again surrounded by a great crowd who were faint and hungry, and had been with him for three days eating little, he took from his disciples seven loaves and a few fish, and again divided them among the people who were four thousand in number. They all ate, and had enough; of what was left, there were gathered up seven baskets full.

He now divided the disciples, and sent them into many towns and villages, teaching the people, and giving them power to cure, in the name of God, all those were ill. And at this time He began to tell them (for he knew what would happen) that he must one day go back to Jerusalem where he would suffer a great deal, and where he would certainly be put to Death. But he said to them that on the third day after he was dead, he would rise from the grave, and ascend to Heaven, where he would sit at the right hand of God, beseeching God's pardon to sinners.

THE LIFE OF OUR LORD

And immediately Jesus stretched forth his hand, and caught him, and said unto him, O thou of little faith, wherefore didst thou doubt? (Matthew 14:31)

Discussion Question:
Are you ever discouraged by the wickedness around you and think that you cannot go on?

December 10

SIX DAYS AFTER THE last Miracle of the loaves and fish, Jesus Christ went up into a high Mountain, with only three of the Disciples—Peter, James, and John. And while he was speaking to them there, suddenly His face began to shine as if it were the Sun, and the robes he wore, which were white, glistened and shone like sparkling silver, and he stood before them like an angel. A bright cloud overshadowed them at the same time; and a voice, speaking from the cloud, was heard to say "This is my beloved Son in whom I am well pleased. Hear ye him!" At which the three disciples fell on their knees and covered their faces; being afraid.

This is called the Transfiguration of our Savior.

When they were come down from this mountain, and were among the people again, a man knelt at the feet of Jesus Christ, and said, "Lord have mercy on my son, for he is mad and cannot help himself, and sometimes falls into the fire, and sometimes into the water, and covers himself with scars and sores. Some of Thy Disciples have tried to cure him, but could not." Our Savior cured the child immediately; and turning to his disciples told them they had not been able to cure him themselves, because they did not believe in Him so truly as he had hoped.

The Disciples asked him, "Master, who is greatest in the Kingdom of Heaven?" Jesus called a little child to him, and took him in his arms, and stood him among them, and answered, "a child like this. I say unto you that none but those who are as humble as little children shall enter into Heaven. Whosoever shall receive one such little child in my name receiveth me. But whosoever hurts one of them, it were better for him that he had a millstone tied about his neck, and were drowned in the depths of the sea. The angels are all children." Our Savior loved the child, and loved all children. Yes, and all the world. No one ever loved all people so well and so truly as He did.

Peter asked Him, "Lord, How often shall I forgive anyone who offends me? Seven times?"

Our Savior answered "Seventy time seven times, and more than that. For how can you hope that God will forgive you, when you do wrong, unless you forgive all other people!"

And he told his disciples this Story—He said, there was once a Servant who owed his master a great deal of money, and could not pay it, at which the Master, being very angry, was going to have this servant sold for a Slave. But the servant kneeling down and begging his Master's pardon with great sorrow, the Master forgave him. Now this same servant had a fellow servant who owed him a hundred pence, and instead of being kind and forgiving to this poor man, as his Master had been to him, he put him in prison for the debt. His master hearing of it, went to him, and said "oh wicked Servant, I forgave you. Why did you not forgive your fellow servant!" And because he had not done so, his Master turned him away with great misery. "So," said Our Savior; "how can you expect God to forgive you, if you do not forgive others!" This is the meaning of that part of the Lord's prayer, where we say "as we forgive us our trespasses"—that word means faults—"as we forgive them that trespass against us."

THE LIFE OF OUR LORD

But Jesus said, Suffer little children, and forbid them not, to come unto me: for of such is the kingdom of heaven. (Matthew 19:14)

Discussion Question:
Why is it so much easier for us to see others' faults than our own?

December 11

AND HE TOLD THEM another story, and said "There was a certain Farmer once, who had a vineyard and he went out early in the morning and agreed with some laborers to work there all day, for a Penny. And by and by, when it was later, he went out again and engaged some more laborers on the same terms; and by and by went out again; and so on, several times, until the afternoon. When the day was over, and they all came to be paid, those who had worked since morning complained that those who had not begun to work until late in the day had the same money as themselves, and they said it was not fair. But the Master, said, "Friend, I agreed with you for a Penny; and is it less money to you, because I give the same money to another man?"

THE LIFE OF OUR LORD

Our Savior meant to teach them by this, that people who have done good all their lives long, will go to Heaven after they are dead. But that people who have been wicked, because of their being miserable, or not having parents and friends to take care of them when young, and who are truly sorry for it, however late in their lives, and pray God to forgive them, will be forgiven and will go to Heaven too. He taught His disciples in these stories, because he knew the people liked to hear them, and would remember what He said better, if he said it in that way. They are called Parables—and I wish you to remember that word, as I shall soon have some more of these Parables to tell you about.

The people listened to all that our Savior said, but were not agreed among themselves about Him. The Pharisees and Jews had spoken to some of them against Him, and some of them were inclined to do Him harm and even to murder Him. But they were afraid, as yet, to do Him any harm, because of His goodness, and His looking so divine and grand—although he was very simply dressed; almost like the poor people—that they could hardly bear to meet his eyes.

One morning, He was sitting in a place called the Mount of Olives, teaching the people who were all clustered round Him, listening and learning attentively, when a great noise was heard, and a crowd of Pharisees, and some other people like them, called Scribes, came running in, with great cries and shouts, dragging among them a woman who had done wrong, and they all cried out together, "Master! Look at this woman. The law says she shall be pelted with stones until she is dead. But what say you? What say you?"

Jesus looked upon the noisy crowd attentively, and knew that they had come to make him say the law was wrong and cruel; and that if He said so, they would make it a charge against Him and would kill him. They were ashamed and afraid as He looked into their faces, but they still cried out, "Come! What say you Master? What say you?"

Jesus stooped down, and wrote with his finger in the sand on the ground, "He that is without sin among you, let him throw the first stone at her." As they read this looking over one another's shoulders, and as He repeated the words to them, they went away, one by one, ashamed, until not a man of all the noisy crowd was left there; and Jesus Christ, and the woman, hiding her face in her hands, alone remained.

Then said Jesus Christ, "Woman, where are thine accusers? Hath no man condemned

THE LIFE OF OUR LORD

Thee?" She answered, trembling, "No Lord!" Then said our Savior, "Neither do I condemn Thee. Go! And sin no more!"

So when they continued asking him, he lifted up himself, and said unto them, He that is without sin among you, let him first cast a stone at her. (John 8:7)

Discussion Question:
Why didn't any of the people stone the woman taken in sin?

December 12

As Our Savior sat teaching the people and answering their questions, a certain Lawyer stood up, and said "Master what shall I do, that I may live again in happiness after I am dead?" Jesus said to him "The first of all the commandments is, the Lord our God is one Lord: and Thou shalt love the Lord Thy God with all Thy heart, and with all Thy mind, and with all thy Strength. And the second is like unto it. Thou shalt love thy neighbor as thyself. There is none other commandment greater than these."

Then the Lawyer said "But who is my neighbor? Tell me that I may know." Jesus answered in this Parable:

"There was once a traveler," he said, "journeying from Jerusalem to Jericho, who fell among Thieves; and they robbed him of his clothes, and wounded him, and went away,

THE LIFE OF OUR LORD

leaving him half dead upon the road. A Priest, happening to pass that way, while the poor man lay there, saw him, but took no notice, and passed by, on the other side. Another man, a Levite, came that way, and also saw him; but he only looked at him for a moment, and then passed by, also. But a certain Samaritan who came traveling along that road, no sooner saw him than he had compassion on him, and dressed his wounds with oil and wine, and set him on the beast he rode himself, and took him to an Inn, and next morning took out of his pocket Two pence and gave them to the Landlord, saying "take care of him and whatever you may spend beyond this, in doing so, I will repay you when I come here again."— Now which of these three men," said our Savior to the Lawyer, "do you think should be called the neighbor of him who fell among the Thieves?" The Lawyer said, "The man who shewed compassion on him." "True," replied our Savior. "Go Thou and do likewise! Be compassionate to all men. For all men are your neighbors and brothers."

And he told them this Parable, of which the meaning is, that we are never to be proud, or think ourselves very good, before God, but are always to be humble. He said, "when you are invited to a Feast or Wedding, do not sit down in the best place, lest some more honored man should come, and claim that seat. But sit down in the lowest place, and a better will be offered you if you deserve it. For whosoever exalteth himself shall be abased, and whosoever humbleth himself shall be exalted."

He also told them this Parable: "There was a certain man who prepared a great supper, and invited many people, and sent his Servant round to them when supper was ready to tell them they were waited for. Upon this, they made excuses. One said he had bought a piece of ground and must go to look at it. Another that he had bought five yoke of Oxen, and must go to try them. Another, that he was newly married, and could not come. When the Master of the house heard this, he was angry, and told the servant to go into the streets, and into the high roads, and among the hedges, and invite the poor, the lame, the maimed, and the blind to supper instead."

The meaning of Our Savior in telling them this Parable, was, that those who are too busy with their own profits and pleasures, to think of God and doing good, will not find such favor with him as the sick and miserable.

THE LIFE OF OUR LORD

And the second is like, namely this, Thou shalt love thy neighbor as thyself. There is none other commandment greater than these. (Mark 12:31)

Discussion Question:
How can we show more love for our neighbors?

December 13

IT HAPPENED THAT OUR Savior, being in the city of Jericho, saw, looking down upon him over the heads of the crowd, from a tree into which he had climbed for that purpose, a man named Zacchaeus, who was regarded as a common kind of man, and a Sinner, but to whom Jesus Christ called out, as He passed along, that He would come and eat with him in his house that day. Those proud men, the Pharisees and Scribes, hearing this, muttered among themselves, and said "he eats with Sinners." In answer to them, Jesus related this Parable, which is usually called THE PARABLE OF THE PRODIGAL SON.

"There was once a Man," he told them, "who had two sons: and the younger of them said one day, "Father, give me my share of your riches now, and let me do with it what I please?" The father granting his request, he

THE LIFE OF OUR LORD

traveled away with his money into a distant country, and soon spent it in riotous living.

When he had spent all, there came a time, through all that country, of great public distress and famine, when there was no bread, and when the corn, and the grass, and all the things that grow in the ground were all dried up and blighted. The Prodigal Son fell into such distress and hunger, that he hired himself out as a servant to feed swine in the fields. And he would have been glad to eat, even the poor coarse husks that the swine were fed with, but his Master gave him none. In this distress, he said to himself "How many of my father's servants have bread enough, and to spare, while I perish with hunger! I will arise and go to my father, and will say unto him, Father! I have sinned against Heaven, and before thee, and am no more worthy to be called Thy Son!"

And so he traveled back again, in great pain and sorrow and difficulty, to his father's house. When he was yet a great way off, his father saw him, and knew him in the midst of all his rags and misery, and ran towards him, and wept, and fell upon his neck, and kissed him. And he told his servants to clothe his poor repentant Son in the best robes, and to make a great feast to celebrate his return. Which was done; and they began to be merry.

But the eldest Son, who had been in the field and knew nothing of his brother's return, coming to the house and hearing the music and Dancing, called to one of the Servants, and asked him what it meant. To this the Servant made answer that his brother had come home, and that his father was joyful because of his return. At this, the elder brother was angry and would not go into the house; so the father, hearing of it, came out to persuade him.

"Father," said the elder brother, "you do not treat me justly, to shew so much joy for my younger brother's return. For these many years I have remained with you constantly, and have been true to you, yet you have never made a feast for me. But when my younger brother returns, who has been prodigal, and riotous, and spent his money in many bad ways, you are full of delight, and the whole house makes merry!"—"Son" returned the father, "you have always been with me, and all I have is yours. But we thought your brother dead, and he is alive. He was lost, and he is found; and it is natural and right that we should be merry for his unexpected return to his old home."

By this, our Savior meant to teach, that those who have done wrong and forgotten God, are always welcome to him and will always receive his mercy, if they will only return to Him in sorrow for the sin of which they have been guilty.

For this my son was dead, and is alive again; he was lost, and is found. And they began to be merry. (Luke 15:24)

Discussion Question:
Does it matter to God whether we have made a big sin or a small sin, if we have repented?

December 14

NOW THE PHARISEES RECEIVED these lessons from our Savior, scornfully; for they were rich, and covetous, and thought themselves superior to all mankind. As a warning to them, Christ related this Parable:—OF DIVES AND LAZARUS.

There was a certain man who was clothed in purple and fine linen, and fared sumptuously every day. And there was a certain beggar, named Lazarus, who was laid at his gate, full of sores and desiring to be fed with crumbs which fell from the rich man's table. Moreover, the dogs came and licked his sores.

And it came to pass that the Beggar died, and was carried by the angels into Abraham's bosom—Abraham had been a very good man who lived many years before that time, and was then in Heaven. The rich man also died, and was buried. And in Hell, he lifted up his eyes, being in torments, and saw Abraham afar off, and Lazarus. And he cried and said, "Father Abraham have mercy on me, and send Lazarus that he may dip the tip of his finger in water and cool my tongue, for I am tormented in this flame." But Abraham said, "Son, remember that in thy lifetime thou receivedst good things, and likewise Lazarus evil things. But now, he is comforted, and thou art tormented!"

And among other Parables, Christ said to these same Pharisees, because of their pride, That two men once went up into the Temple, to pray; of whom, one was a Pharisee, and one a Publican. The Pharisee said, "God I thank Thee, that I am not unjust as other men are, or bad as this Publican is!" The Publican, standing afar off, would not lift up his eyes to Heaven, but struck his breast, and only said, "God be merciful to me, a Sinner!" And God,—our Savior told them—would be merciful to that man rather than the other, and would be better pleased with his prayer, because he made it with a humble and lowly heart.

The Pharisees were so angry at being taught these things, that they employed some spies to ask Our Savior questions, and try to entrap Him into saying something which was against the Law. The Emperor of that country, who was called Caesar, having commanded tribute money to be regularly paid to him by the people, and being cruel against any one who disputed his right to it, these spies thought they might, perhaps, induce our Savior to say it was an unjust payment, and so to bring himself under the Emperor's displeasure. Therefore, pretending to be very humble, they came to Him and said, "Master you teach the word of God rightly, and do not respect persons on account of their wealth or high station. Tell us, is it lawful that we should pay tribute to Caesar?"

Christ, who knew their thoughts, replied, "Why do you ask? Shew me a penny." They did so. "Whose image, and whose name, is this upon it?" he asked them. They said "Caesar's." "Then," said He, "Render unto Caesar, the things that are Caesar's."

So they left him; very much enraged and disappointed that they could not entrap Him. But our Savior knew their hearts and thoughts, as well as He knew that other men were conspiring against him, and that he would soon be put to Death.

As he was teaching them thus, he sat near the Public Treasury, where people as they passed along the street, were accustomed to drop money into a box for the poor; and many rich persons, passing while Jesus sat there, had put in a great deal of money. At last there came a poor Widow who dropped in two mites, each half a farthing in value, and then went quietly away. Jesus, seeing her do this as he rose to leave the place, called his disciples about him, and said to them that that poor widow had been more truly charitable than all the rest who had given money that day; for the others were rich and would never miss what they had given, but she was very poor, and had given those two mites which might have bought her bread to eat.

Let us never forget what the poor widow did, when we think we are charitable.

And he said unto them, Render therefore unto Caesar the things which be Caesar's, and unto God the things which be God's. (Luke 20:25)

Discussion Question:
Who was the widow giving her money to? How can we be more charitable in our lives?

December 15

THERE WAS A CERTAIN man named Lazarus of Bethany, who was taken very ill; and as he was the Brother of that Mary who had anointed Christ with ointment, and wiped his feet with her hair, She and her sister Martha sent to him in great trouble, saying, Lord, Lazarus whom you love is sick, and like to die.

Jesus did not go to them for two days after receiving this message; but when that time was past, he said to his Disciples, "Lazarus is dead. Let us go to Bethany." When they arrived there (it was a place very near to Jerusalem) they found, as Jesus had foretold, that Lazarus was dead, and had been dead and buried, four days.

When Martha heard that Jesus was coming, she rose up from among the people who had come to condole with her on her poor brother's death, and ran to meet him: leaving her sister

THE LIFE OF OUR LORD

Mary weeping, in the house. When Martha saw Him she burst into tears, and said "Oh Lord if Thou hadst been here, my brother would not have died."—"Thy brother shall rise again," returned Our Savior. "I know he will, and I believe he will, Lord, at the Resurrection on the Last Day," said Martha.

Jesus said to her, "I am the Resurrection and the Life. Dost thou believe this?" She answered "Yes Lord;" and running back to her sister Mary, told her that Christ was come. Mary hearing this, ran out, followed by all those who had been grieving with her in the house, and coming to the place where he was, fell down at his feet upon the ground and wept; and so did all the rest. Jesus was so full of compassion for their sorrow, that He wept too, as he said, "Where have you laid him?"—They said, "Lord, come and see!"

He was buried in a cave; and there was a great stone laid upon it. When they all came to the Grave, Jesus ordered the stone to be rolled away, which was done. Then, after casting up his eyes, and thanking God, he said, in a loud and solemn voice, "Lazarus, come forth!" and the dead man, Lazarus, restored to life, came out among the people, and went home with his sisters. At this sight, so awful and affecting, many of the people there, believed that Christ was indeed the Son of God; come to instruct and save mankind. But others ran to tell the Pharisees; and from that day the Pharisees resolved among themselves—to prevent more people from believing in him, that Jesus should be killed. And they agreed among themselves—meeting in the Temple for that purpose—that if he came into Jerusalem before the Feast of the Passover, which was then approaching, he should be seized.

It was six days before the Passover, when Jesus raised Lazarus from the dead; and, at night, when they all sat at supper together, with Lazarus among them, Mary rose up, and took a pound of ointment (which was very precious and costly, and was called ointment of Spikenard) and anointed the feet of Jesus Christ with it, and, once again, wiped them on her hair; and the whole house was filled with the pleasant smell of the ointment. Judas Iscariot, one of the Disciples, pretended to be angry at this, and said that the ointment might have been sold for Three Hundred Pence, and the money given to the poor. But he only said so, in reality, because he carried the Purse, and was (unknown to the rest, at that time) a Thief, and wished to get all the money he could. He now began to plot for betraying Christ into the hands of the Chief Priests.

Jesus wept. Then said the Jews, Behold how he loved him! (John 11:35)

Discussion Question:
Why would the Pharisees refuse to accept that Jesus had power from God after raising Lazarus from the dead?

December 16

THE FEAST OF THE Passover now drawing very near, Jesus Christ, with his disciples, moved forward toward Jerusalem. When they were come near to that city, He pointed to a village and told two of his disciples to go there, and they would find an ass, with a colt, tied to a tree, which they were to bring to Him. Finding these animals exactly as Jesus had described, they brought them away, and Jesus, riding on the ass, entered Jerusalem. An immense crowd of people collected round him as he went along, and throwing their robes on the ground, and cutting down green branches from the trees, and spreading them in His path, they shouted, and cried 'Hosanna to the Son of David!' (David had been a great King there) "He comes in the name of the Lord! This is Jesus, the Prophet of Nazareth!" And when Jesus went into the

Temple, and cast out the tables of the money-changers who wrongfully sat there, together with people who sold Doves; saying "My father's house is a house of prayer, but ye have made it a den of Thieves!"—and when the people and children cried in the Temple "This is Jesus the Prophet of Nazareth," and would not be silenced—and when the blind and lame came flocking there in crowds, and were healed by his hand—the Chief Priests and Scribes, and Pharisees were filled with fear and hatred of Him. But Jesus continued to heal the sick, and to do good, and went and lodged at Bethany; a place that was very near the City of Jerusalem, but not within the walls.

One night, at that place, he rose from Supper at which he was seated with his Disciples, and taking a cloth and a basin of water, washed their feet. Simon Peter, one of the Disciples, would have prevented Him from washing his feet: but our Savior told Him that He did this, in order that they, remembering it, might be always kind and gentle to one another, and might know no pride or ill-will among themselves.

Then, he became sad, and grieved, and looking round on the Disciples said, "There is one here, who will betray me." They cried out, one after another, "Is it I, Lord!—Is it I!" But he only answered, "It is one of the Twelve that dippeth with me in the dish." One of the disciples, whom Jesus loved, happening to be leaning on His Breast at that moment listening to his words, Simon Peter beckoned to him that he should ask the name of this false man. Jesus answered "It is he to whom I shall give a sop when I have dipped it in the dish" and when he had dipped it, He gave it to Judas Iscariot, saying "What thou doest, do quickly." Which the other disciples did not understand, but which Judas knew to mean that Christ had read his bad thoughts.

So Judas, taking the sop, went out immediately. It was night, and he went straight to the chief Priests and said "what will you give me, if I deliver him to you?" They agreed to give him thirty pieces of Silver; and for this, he undertook soon to betray into their hands, his Lord and Master Jesus Christ.

A new commandment I give unto you, That ye love one another; as I have loved you, that ye also love one another. (John 13:34)

Discussion Question:
How can we follow Jesus' example of service?

December 17

FEAST OF THE PASSOVER being almost come, Jesus said to two of His Disciples, Peter and John, "Go into the city of Jerusalem, and you will meet a man carrying a pitcher of water. Follow him home, and say to him, 'The Master says, where is the guest chamber, where He can eat the Passover with His Disciples?' and he will show you a large upper room, furnished. There make ready the supper."

The two Disciples found that it happened as Jesus had said; and having met the man with the pitcher of water, and having followed him home, and having been shown the room, they prepared the supper, and Jesus and the other ten Apostles came at the usual time, and they all sat down to partake of it together.

It is always called the Last Supper, because this was the last time that Our Savior ate and drank with His Disciples.

And He took bread from the table, and blessed it, and broke it, and gave it to them; and He took the cup of wine, and blessed it, and drank, and gave it to them, saying, "Do this in remembrance of me!" And when they had finished supper, and had sung a hymn, they went out into the Mount of Olives.

There, Jesus told them, that He would be seized that night, and that they would all leave Him alone, and would think only of their own safety. Peter said, earnestly, he never would, for one. "Before the cock crows," returned Our Savior, "you will deny me thrice." But Peter answered, "No, Lord. Though I should die with Thee, I will never deny Thee." And all the other Disciples said the same.

Jesus then led the way over a brook, called Cedron, into a garden that was called Gethsemane; and walked with three of the Disciples into a retired part of the garden. Then He left them as He had left the others, together; saying, "Wait here, and watch!" and went away and prayed by Himself, while they, being weary, fell asleep.

And Christ suffered great sorrow and distress of mind, in His prayers in that garden,

THE LIFE OF OUR LORD

because of the wickedness of the men of Jerusalem who were going to kill Him; and He shed tears before God, and was in deep and strong affliction.

When His prayers were finished, and He was comforted, He returned to the Disciples, and said, "Rise! Let us be going! He is close at hand, who will betray me!"

Now, Judas knew that garden well, for Our Savior had often walked there with His Disciples; and, almost at the moment when Our Savior said these words, he came there, accompanied by a strong guard of men and officers, which had been sent by the chief priests and Pharisees. It being dark, they carried lanterns and torches. They were armed with swords and staves too; for they did not know but that the people would rise and defend Jesus Christ; and this had made them afraid to seize Him boldly in the day, when He sat teaching the people.

As the leaders of this guard had never seen Jesus Christ and did not know Him from the Apostles, Judas had said to them, "The man whom I kiss, will be He." As he advanced to give this wicked kiss, Jesus said to the soldiers, "Whom do you seek?" "Jesus of Nazareth," they answered. "Then," said Our Savior, "I am He, Let my Disciples here go freely. I am He."

Which Judas confirmed, by saying, "Hail Master!" and kissing Him. Whereupon Jesus said, "Judas, thou betrayest me with a kiss!" The guard then ran forward to seize Him. No one offered to protect Him, except Peter, who, having a sword, drew it, and cut off the right ear of the high priest's servant, who was one of them, and whose name was Malchus. But Jesus made him sheathe his sword, and gave Himself up. Then, all the Disciples forsook Him and fled; and there remained not one not one to bear Him company.

And he took bread, and gave thanks, and brake it, and gave unto them, saying, This is my body which is given for you: this do in remembrance of me. (Luke 22:19)

Discussion Question:
What did Jesus want us to remember in partaking of his sacraments?

December 18

AFTER A SHORT TIME, Peter and another Disciple took heart, and secretly followed the guard to the house of Caiaphas the High Priest, whither Jesus was taken, and where the Scribes and others were assembled to question Him. Peter stood at the door, but the other disciple, who was known to the High Priest, went in, and presently returning, asked the woman, who kept the door, to admit Peter too. She, looking at him said, "Are you not one of the Disciples?" He said, "I am not." So she let him in; and he stood before a fire that was there, warming himself, among the servants and officers who were crowded round it. For it was very cold.

Some of these men asked him the same question as the woman had done, and said, "Are you not one of the disciples?" He again denied it, and said, "I am not." One of them, who was related to that man whose ear Peter had cut off with his sword, said "Did I not see you in the garden with him?" Peter again denied it with an oath, and said, "I do not know the man." Immediately the cock crew, and Jesus turning round, looked steadfastly at Peter. Then Peter remembered what He had said—that before the cock crew, he would deny Him thrice—and went out, and wept bitterly.

Among other questions that were put to Jesus, the High Priest asked Him what He had taught the people. To which He answered that He had taught them in the open day, and in the open streets, and that the priests should ask the people what they had learned of Him. One of the officers struck Jesus with his hand for this reply; and two false witnesses coming in, said they had heard Him say that He could destroy the Temple of God and build it again in three days. Jesus answered little; but the Scribes and Priests agreed that He was guilty of blasphemy, and should be put to death; and they spat upon, and beat him.

When Judas Iscariot saw that His Master was indeed condemned, he was so full of horror for what he had done, that he took the Thirty Pieces of Silver back to the Chief Priests, and said "I have betrayed innocent blood! I cannot keep it!" with those words, he threw the money

THE LIFE OF OUR LORD

down upon the floor, and rushing away, wild with despair, hanged himself. The rope, being weak, broke with the weight of his body, and it fell down on the ground, after Death, all bruised and burst,—a dreadful sight to see! The chief Priests, not knowing what else to do with the Thirty Pieces of Silver, bought a burying place for strangers with it, the proper name of which was The Potters' Field. But the people called it The Field of Blood ever afterward.

And Simon Peter stood and warmed himself. They said therefore unto him, Art not thou also one of his disciples? He denied it, and said, I am not. (John 18:25)

Discussion Question:
How can we show through our actions that we are disciples of Christ?

December 19

JESUS WAS TAKEN FROM the High Priests' to the Judgment Hall where Pontius Pilate, the Governor, sat, to administer Justice. Pilate (who was not a Jew) said to Him "your own Nation, the Jews, and your own Priests have delivered you to me. What have you done?" Finding that He had done no harm, Pilate went out and told the Jews so; but they said "He has been teaching the People what is not true and what is wrong; and he began to do so, long ago, in Galilee." As Herod had the right to punish people who offended against the law in Galilee, Pilate said, "I find no wrong in him. Let him be taken before Herod!"

They carried Him accordingly before Herod, where he sat surrounded by his stern soldiers and men in armor. And these laughed at, Jesus, and dressed him, in mockery, in a fine robe, and sent him back to Pilate. And Pilate called the Priests and People together again, and said "I find no wrong in this man; neither does Herod. He has done nothing to deserve death." But they cried out, "He has, he has! Yes, yes! Let him be killed!"

Pilate was troubled in his mind to hear them so clamorous against Jesus Christ. His wife, too, had dreamed all night about it, and sent to him upon the Judgment Seat saying "Have nothing to do with that just man!" As it was the custom of the feast of the Passover to give some prisoner his liberty, Pilate endeavored to persuade the people to ask for the release of Jesus. But they said (being very ignorant and passionate, and being told to do so, by the Priests) "No, no, we will not have him released. Release Barabbas, and let this man be crucified!"

Barabbas was a wicked criminal, in jail for his crimes, and in danger of being put to death.

Pilate, finding the people so determined against Jesus, delivered him to the soldiers to be scourged—that is beaten. They plaited a crown of thorns, and put it on his head, and dressed Him in a purple robe, and spat upon him, and struck him with their hands, and said "Hail, King of the Jews!"—remembering that the crowd had called him the Son of David when he entered into Jerusalem. And they ill-used him in many cruel ways; but Jesus bore it patiently, and only said "Father! Forgive them! They know not what they do!"

Once more, Pilate brought Him out before the people, dressed in the purple robe and crown of thorns, and said "Behold the man!" They cried out, savagely, "Crucify him! Crucify him!" So did the chief Priests and officers. "Take him and crucify him yourselves," said Pilate. "I find no fault in him." But they cried out, "He called himself the Son of God; and that, by the Jewish Law is Death! And he called himself King of the Jews; and that is against the Roman Law, for we have no King but Caesar, who is the Roman Emperor. If you let him go, you are not Caesar's friend. Crucify him! Crucify him!"

When Pilate saw that he could not prevail with them, however hard he tried, he called for water, and washing his hands before the crowd, said, "I am innocent of the blood of this just person." Then he delivered Him to them to be crucified; and they, shouting and gathering round Him, and treating him (who still prayed for them to God) with cruelty and insult, took Him away.

THE LIFE OF OUR LORD

Pilate therefore went forth again, and saith unto them, Behold, I bring him forth to you, that ye may know that I find no fault in him. (John 19:4)

Discussion Question:
Was Pilate able to wash away the guilt for his part in the crucifixion by washing his hands in this way?

December 20

THAT YOU MAY KNOW what the People meant when they said "Crucify him!" I must tell you that in those times, which were very cruel times indeed (let us thank God and Jesus Christ that they are past!) it was the custom to kill people who were sentenced to Death, by nailing them alive on a great wooden Cross, planted upright in the ground, and leaving them there, exposed to the Sun and Wind, and day and night, until they died of pain and thirst. It was the custom too, to make them walk to the place of execution, carrying the cross-piece of wood to which their hands were to be afterward nailed; that their shame and suffering might be the greater.

Bearing his Cross, upon his shoulder, like the commonest and most wicked criminal, our blessed Savior, Jesus Christ, surrounded by the persecuting crowd, went out of Jerusalem to a place called in the Hebrew language, Golgotha; that is, the place of a skull. And being come to a hill called Mount Calvary, they hammered cruel nails through his hands and feet and nailed him on the Cross, between two other crosses on each of which, a common thief was nailed in agony. Over His head, they fastened this writing "Jesus of Nazareth, the King of the Jews"—in three languages; in Hebrew, in Greek, and in Latin.

Meantime, a guard of four soldiers, sitting on the ground, divided His clothes (which they had taken off) into four parcels for themselves, and cast lots for His coat, and sat there, gambling and talking, while He suffered. They offered him vinegar to drink, mixed with gall; and wine, mixed with myrrh, but he took none.[34] And the wicked people who passed that way, mocked him, and said "If Thou be the Son of God, come down from the cross." The Chief Priests also mocked Him, and said "He came to save Sinners. Let him save himself!" One of the Thieves too, railed at him, in his torture, and said, "If Thou be Christ, save thyself, and us." But the other Thief, who was penitent, said "Lord! Remember me when Thou comest into

---

[34] Thought to be narcotic to dull Jesus' senses.

Thy Kingdom!" And Jesus answered, " Today, thou shalt be with me in Paradise."

None were there, to take pity on Him, but one disciple and four women. God blessed those women for their true and tender hearts! They were, the mother of Jesus, his mother's sister, Mary, the wife of Cleophas, and Mary Magdalene who had twice dried his feet upon her hair. The disciple was he whom Jesus loved—John, who had leaned upon his breast and asked Him which was the Betrayer. When Jesus saw them standing at the foot of the Cross, He said to His mother that John would be her son, to comfort her when He was dead; and from that hour John was as a son to her, and loved her.

When Jesus therefore saw his mother, and the disciple standing by, whom he loved, he saith unto his mother, Woman, behold thy son! (John 19:26)

Discussion Question:
Why did Jesus not save himself from the cross?

December 21

AT ABOUT THE SIXTH hour, a deep and terrible darkness came over all the land, and lasted until the ninth hour, when Jesus cried out, with a loud voice, "My God, My God, why has Thou forsaken me!" The soldiers, hearing him, dipped a sponge in some vinegar, that was standing there, and fastening it to long reed, put it up to His Mouth. When He had received it, He said "It is finished!"—And crying "Father! Into thy hands I commend my Spirit!"—died.

Then, there was a dreadful earthquake; and the Great wall of the Temple, cracked; and the rocks were rent asunder. The guard, terrified at these sights, said to each other, "Surely this was the Son of God!"—and the People who had been watching the cross from a distance (among whom were many women) smote upon their breasts, and went fearfully and sadly, home.

The next day, being the Sabbath, the Jews were anxious that the Bodies should be taken down at once, and made that request to Pilate. Therefore some soldiers came, and broke the legs of the two criminals to kill them; but coming to Jesus, and finding Him already dead, they only pierced his side with a spear. From the wound, there came out, blood and water.

There was a good man named Joseph of Arimathea—a Jewish City—who believed in Christ, and going to Pilate privately (for fear of the Jews) begged that he might have the body. Pilate consenting, he and one Nicodemus, rolled it in linen and spices—it was the custom of the Jews to prepare bodies for burial in that way—and buried it in a new tomb or sepulcher, which had been cut out of a rock in a garden near to the place of Crucifixion, and where no one had ever yet been buried. They then rolled a great stone to the mouth of the sepulcher, and left Mary Magdalene, and the other Mary, sitting there, watching it.

The Chief Priests and Pharisees remembering that Jesus Christ had said to his disciples that He would rise from the grave on the third day after His death, went to Pilate and prayed that the Sepulcher might be well taken care off until that day, lest the disciples should steal the Body, and afterwards say to the people that Christ was risen from the dead. Pilate agreeing to this, a guard of soldiers was set over it constantly, and the stone was sealed up besides. And so it remained, watched and sealed, until the third day; which was the first day of the week.

When that morning began to dawn, Mary Magdalene and the other Mary, and some other women, came to the Sepulcher, with some more spices which they had prepared. As they were saying to each other, "How shall we roll away the stone?" the earth trembled and shook, and an angel, descending from Heaven, rolled it back, and then sat resting on it. His countenance was like lightning, and his garments were white as snow; and at sight of him, the men of the guard fainted away with fear, as if they were dead.

Now when the centurion saw what was done, he glorified God, saying, Certainly this was a righteous man. (Luke 23:47)

Discussion Question:
What made the soldiers believe Jesus was the Son of God? What is it that makes us believe?

December 22

MARY MAGDALENE SAW THE stone rolled away, and waiting to see no more, ran to Peter and John who were coming towards the place, and said "They have taken away the Lord and we know not where they have laid him!" They immediately ran to the Tomb, but John, being the faster of the two, outran the other, and got there first. He stooped down, and looked in, and saw the linen cloths in which the body had been wrapped, lying there; but he did not go in. When Peter came up, he went in, and saw the linen clothes lying in one place, and a napkin that had been bound about the head, in another. John also went in then, and saw the same things. Then they went home, to tell the rest.

But Mary Magdalene remained outside the sepulcher, weeping. After a little time, she stooped down, and looked in, and saw Two angels, clothed in white, sitting where the body of Christ had lain. These said to her, "Woman, why weepest Thou?" She answered, "Because they have taken away my Lord, and I know not where they have laid him." As she gave this answer, she turned round, and saw Jesus standing behind her, but did not Then know Him. "Woman," said He, "Why weepest thou? What seekest thou?" She, supposing Him to be the gardener, replied, "Sir! If thou hast borne my Lord hence, tell me where Thou hast laid him, and I will take him away." Jesus pronounced her name, "Mary." Then she knew him, and, starting, exclaimed "Master!"—"Touch me not," said Christ; "for I am not yet ascended to my father; but go to my disciples, and say unto them, I ascend unto my Father, and your Father; and to my God, and to your God!"

Accordingly, Mary Magdalene went and told the Disciples that she had seen Christ, and what He had said to her; and with them she found the other women whom she had left at the Sepulcher when she had gone to call those two disciples Peter and John. These women told her and the rest, that they had seen at the Tomb, two men in shining garments, at sight of whom they had been afraid, and had bent down, but who had told them that the Lord was risen; and also that as they came to tell this, they had seen Christ, on the way, and had held him by the feet, and worshipped Him. But these accounts seemed to the apostles at that time, as idle tales, and they did not believe them.

The soldiers of the guard too, when they recovered from their fainted-fit, and went to the Chief Priests to tell them what they had seen, were silenced with large sums of money, and were told by them to say that the Disciples had stolen the Body away while they were asleep.

Go to my brethren, and say unto them, I ascend unto my Father, and your Father; and to my God, and your God. (John 20:17)

Discussion Question:
Why do you think Christ appeared first to Mary and not to the disciples?

December 23

BUT IT HAPPENED THAT on that same day, Simon and Cleopas—Simon one of the twelve Apostles, and Cleopas one of the followers of Christ were walking to a village called Emmaus, at some little distance from Jerusalem, and were talking, by the way, upon the death and resurrection of Christ, when they were joined by a stranger, who explained the Scriptures to them, and told them a great deal about God, so that they wondered at his knowledge. As the night was fast coming on when they reached the village, they asked this stranger to stay with them, which he consented to do. When they all three sat down to supper, he took some bread, and blessed it, and broke it as Christ had done at the Last Supper. Looking on him in wonder they found that his face was changed before them, and that it was Christ himself; and as they looked on him, he disappeared.

They instantly rose up, and returned to Jerusalem, and finding the disciples sitting together, told them what they had seen. While they were speaking, Jesus suddenly stood in the midst of all the company, and said "Peace be unto ye!" Seeing that they were greatly frightened, he shewed them his hands and feet, and invited them to touch Him; and, to encourage them and give them time to recover themselves, he ate a piece of broiled fish and a piece of honeycomb before them all.

But Thomas, one of the Twelve Apostles, was not there, at that time; and when the rest said to him afterwards, "We have seen the Lord!" he answered "Except I shall see in his hands the print of the nails, and thrust my hand into his side, I will not believe!" At that moment, though the doors were all shut, Jesus again appeared, standing among them, and said "Peace be unto you!" Then He said to Thomas, "Reach hither thy finger, and behold my hands; and reach hither thy hand, and thrust it into my side; and be no longer faithless, but believing." And Thomas answered, and said to him, " My Lord and my God!" Then said Jesus, "Thomas, because thou hast seen me, thou has believed.

Blessed are they that have not seen me, and yet have believed."

After that time, Jesus Christ was seen by five hundred of his followers at once, and He remained with others of them forty days, teaching them, and instructing them to go forth into the world, and preach His gospel and religion; not minding what wicked men might do to them. And conducting his disciples at last, out of Jerusalem as far as Bethany, he blessed them, and ascended in a cloud to Heaven, and took His place at the right hand of God. And while they gazed into the bright blue sky where He had vanished, two white-robed angels appeared among them, and told them that as they had seen Christ ascend to Heaven, so He would, one day, come descending from it, to judge the World.

Jesus saith unto him, Thomas, because thou hast seen me, thou hast believed: blessed are they that have not seen, and yet have believed. (John 20:29)

Discussion Question:
How can we believe when we cannot see and touch Christ like Thomas did?

December 24

HEN CHRIST WAS SEEN no more, the Apostles began to teach the People as He had commanded them. And having chosen a new apostle, named Matthias, to replace the Wicked Judas, they wandered into all countries, telling the People of Christ's Life and Death—and of the Crucifixion and Resurrection—and of the Lessons he had taught—and baptizing them in Christ's name. And through the power He had given them they healed the sick, and gave sight to the Blind, and speech to the Dumb, and Hearing to the Deaf, as he had done. And Peter being thrown into Prison, was delivered from it, in the dead of night, by an Angel: and once, his words before God caused a man named Ananias, and his wife Sapphira, who had told a lie, to be struck down dead, upon the Earth.

Wherever they went, they were persecuted and cruelly treated; and one man named Saul who had held the clothes of some barbarous persons who pelted one of the Christians named Stephen, to death with stones, was always active in doing them harm. But God turned Saul's heart afterwards; for as he was traveling to Damascus to find out some Christians who were there, and drag them to prison, there shone about him a great light from Heaven; a voice cried, "Saul, Saul, why persecutest thou me!" and he was struck down from his horse, by an invisible hand, in sight of all the guards and soldiers who were riding with him. When they raised him, they found that he was blind; and so he remained for three days, neither eating nor drinking, until one of the Christians (sent to him by an angel for that purpose) restored his sight in the name of Jesus Christ. After which, he became a Christian, and preached, and taught, and believed, with the apostles, and did great service.

They took the name of Christians from Our Savior Christ, and carried Crosses as their sign, because upon a Cross He had suffered Death. The religions that were then in the World were false and brutal, and encouraged men to violence. Beasts, and even men, were killed in the churches, in the belief that the smell of their blood was pleasant to the Gods—there were supposed to be a great many Gods—and many most cruel and disgusting ceremonies prevailed. Yet, for all this, and though the Christian Religion was such a true, and kind, and good one, the Priests of the old Religions long persuaded the people to do all possible hurt to the Christians; and Christians were hanged, beheaded, burnt, buried alive, and devoured in Theaters by Wild Beasts for the public amusement, during many years. Nothing would silence them, or terrify them though; for they knew that if they did their duty, they would go to Heaven. So thousands upon thousands of Christians sprung up and taught the people and were cruelly killed, and were succeeded by other Christians, until the Religion gradually became the great religion of the world.

Remember!—It is Christianity TO DO GOOD always—even to those who do evil to us. It is Christianity to love our neighbor as ourself, and to do to all men as we would have them Do to us. It is Christianity to be gentle, merciful, and forgiving, and to keep those qualities quiet in our own hearts, and never make a boast of them, or of our prayers or of our love of God, but always to shew that we love Him by humbly trying to do right in everything. If we do this, and remember the life

THE LIFE OF OUR LORD

and lessons of Our Lord Jesus Christ, and try to act up to them, we may confidently hope that God will forgive us our sins and mistakes, and enable us to live and die in Peace.

And he answering said, Thou shalt love the Lord thy God with all thy heart, and with all thy soul, and with all thy strength, and with all thy mind; and thy neighbor as thyself. (Luke 10:27)

Discussion Question:
What can we do to spread the good news of the gospel of Christ?

~ ~ ~

Written by Charles Dickens for his young children.

What our Lord Jesus Christ taught to His Disciples and to us, and what we should remember every day of our lives, to love the Lord our God with all our heart, and with all our mind, and with all our soul, and with all our strength; to love our neighbors as ourselves, to do unto other people as we would have them do unto us and to be charitable and gentle to all.

CHARLES DICKENS

There is no other commandment, our Lord Jesus Christ said, greater than these.

For the Evening.
O God, who has made everything, and is so kind and merciful to everything He has made, who tries to be good and to deserve it; God bless my dear Papa and Mamma, Brothers and Sisters and all my Relations and Friends. Make me a good little child, and let me never be naughty and tell a lie, which is a mean and shameful thing. Make me kind to my nurses and servants, and to all beggars and poor people, and let me never be cruel to any dumb creatures, for if I am cruel to anything, even to a poor little fly, God, who is so good, will never love me. And pray God to bless and preserve us all, this night, and forevermore, through Jesus Christ our Lord. Amen.

Extension Activities

Here are a few extension activities that you can try, to get your juices flowing. Feel free to add your own ideas!

- Read the four gospels
- Charles Dickens' use of commas is quite different from modern American usage. Copy a paragraph from The Life of Our Lord and standardize the comma usage.
- Read or watch another account of the Nativity (birth of Christ)
- Compare and contrast how your own beliefs are the same as or different than Dickens'
- Perform your own nativity or dramatize another story from the life of Christ

Biography

Charles Dickens is one of the most beloved storytellers from the Victorian Era.

Much of Dickens' work revolves around the plight of the poor during his time. He wasn't just writing about what he had heard. He had experienced much of what he wrote. His father was incarcerated in debtor's prison when Charles was twelve, and Charles was soon forced to go to work to help support the family. He worked ten hour days pasting labels on pots of boot polish. He was greatly affected by his experience there. Much of his life in this time provided the backdrops for his later stories.

He went on to become a reporter and was a great fan of the theatre, and soon became a writer. He wrote fifteen novels and five novellas, and was a vigorous advocate for the rights of children and the poor.

What's Next?

Did you enjoy this book? Reviews and recommendations are vital to making a book successful. Please leave a review at your favorite online book store or review site and share it with your friends.

More Workman Family Classics, other classics, and suspense/young adult fiction books by P.D. Workman can be found at pdworkman.com

Sign up for my mailing list to be notified of new releases by Workman Classic Schoolbooks and P.D. Workman

Made in the USA
Charleston, SC
23 November 2015